THIS IS THE LANGUAGE
THAT WAS GIVEN TO US

T·B·L·R

THE BARE LIFE REVIEW

Founded in 2017 by
David Wystan Owen: Publisher
Nyuol Lueth Tong: Editor-in-Chief
Ellen Namakaokealoha Kamoe: Director of Operations

Published by The Bare Life Review
PO Box 352
Lagunitas, CA 94938

Cover Image: Jehad Saftawi. *What I Love Doing*, 2014. Photograph.
Reproduced by permission of the author.

Printed in The United States by Bookmobile

ISBN: 978-1-7341823-0-9

www.barelifereview.org

The Bare Life Review is a fiscally-sponsored
project of Intersection for the Arts, a 501(c)(3)
nonprofit organization.

MASTHEAD

Co-Founder / Editor-in-Chief   Nyuol Lueth Tong

Fiction Editor   Maria Kuznetsova

Poetry Editor   Rebecca Liu

Non-Fiction Editor   Novuyo Rosa Tshuma

Online Editor   Etan Nechin

Social Media Manager   Safiya Driskell

Editorial Advisory Board   Jordan Bass
                                  Ainehi Edoro
                                  Dave Eggers
                                  Paul Harding
                                  Naomi Jackson
                                  Akhil Sharma

Governing Board   Sam Alcabes
                                  Megan Cummins
                                  Gwen Litvak

Designer   Nate Kauffman

CONTENTS

EDITOR'S NOTE

THIS THIRD VOLUME of The Bare Life Review is the first to carry a title: *This Is the Language That Was Given to Us*, a phrase drawn from Anca Roncea's poem "sound modeling," included in this issue. Given the journal's mission of championing writing by refugees and immigrants, the reader might readily, and perhaps justifiably, take for granted what we mean to indicate by this title. It is true that we are signaling here, as we have done in the past and will continue to insist upon, the existence of a community of writers who share a language derived from their common albeit complex and diverse experiences of displacement, dislocation, dispossession, or migration. To advocate for migrant literature as we do, however, to claim that we share a language, is by no means an affirmation of its autonomy or that it is a discrete entity whose content and shape is immanent and impregnable. That would merely suggest a kind of fatal parochialism, a boundedness that is not true to any literature, really, nor to the work of the refugee and immigrant writers featured here.

So, what *do* we mean by this title? What is this language that was given to us, and by whom or what exactly? Our language is certainly not one. Our contributors come from every corner of the world (such as South Sudan, Mexico, Germany, Jamaica, Taiwan, Iran) with their own native tongues and particular histories, which are confounding even to each other, but that does not mean that, taken together, refugee and immigrant writers constitute a kind of Babel. Or perhaps we do, but not in the proper sense of language. The language that we claim as our shared possession here is a mode of experience and survival, of relating to each other and negotiating our being and becoming wherever we find ourselves bidden by necessity, of 'creative synthesis,' to borrow Alfred North Whitehead's phrase, the aim of which is furnishing our precarious existence in a hostile world.

In other words, our language is our way of living, remembering, dreaming, questioning—of asserting ourselves. Take Anna Andrew's "Five Ways to Eat Termites," for instance. It is a moving chronicle of a refugee's journey from her village in southern Sudan to Uganda, Sudan, and Egypt. The painful vicissitudes of being a refugee are evoked through cooking and food, its scarcity and variety. Hunger itself becomes the very reality of exile. The struggle to find something to eat, that hungering also becomes the deeper hungering for home that plagues the displaced. Anna's recipes and cooking methods are her grammar of persistence, depository of memories and stories, the language that survival has given her. Or Sergio Aguilar Rivera's "Moon Egg," a Kafkaesque evocation of the anxieties that might beset a young mother. Birth, the act of bringing another being into the world, is registered not merely as a natural event but rather an expelling of the soul. But this expelling of the soul should not be read in a negative light; it is an enlargement of the self and, by extension, the world.

In many senses, that rupture, which occasions radical defamiliarization, transformation, and envisagement of new possibilities—and which we see iterated in various forms throughout the work in this issue—is precisely the enduring signature of migrant literature.

Nyuol Lueth Tong
November 1, 2019

Easter Tourist

Namwali Serpell

Maundy Thursday

B ELLS ARE RINGING and I am running. My shoes—cheap flats,
suede, lilac—slap cobblestone, then pavement. To one side of
me is a line of people queuing up for the chapel, staggered to look
ahead like jostled dominoes. To the other side, beyond a low spiky
fence, is the bright untouchable green.

You are not permitted to step on the grass at King's College.
Last night, a brown English woman stood at a podium in the dining hall to testify about breaking this rule. She was playing with her
children when a guard accosted her. "I am a Fellow of the College,"
she'd said evenly to the guard, she repeated evenly to us, still furi-
ous. There was something lurking in the air as she spoke, about the
masculine word "Fellow," but she didn't bother with it, nor with
the heavy portraits of men—only men—on the walls around us. I
found myself staring up, up at the fragile glass windows above—so
old and fragile that a red light buzzes on if it gets too loud in the
dining hall at King's.

The chapel at King's has this ambivalent weight as well: ponderous and delicate at once. And the tree in front of the college has it, too. Its branches, skeletal in the winter, seem to grow down toward the ground then scoop upward from it. We named it Rufus, you and I. A tipsy night, holding gloved hands, walking in step. You pointed and said, "A dog," and I instantly saw it too. A shared delusion.

Spring has come now. Rufus in his garlands. I run past the tree, I run through the gates, I run towards you. I imagine I'm whizzing through the air like a straight arrow, but as I reach the entrance to the chapel—you're at the front of the queue—I see the look on your face and realize that I'm gangling and weak, a child hurling myself into your hug. "Come on," you smile. "We're late."

The inside of the chapel feels high and hollow. We make our way through the long neck of the building. My nose, heated by my run, cooled by the interior, begins its abominable drip. I have a cold. There are crumpled tissues in my pockets, papier-machéd with the glue of me. They'll have to do. We sit along a wall facing those seated against the opposite wall. A strange way to be in a church: staring at the others. Do more people stay focused on God this way, bowing to the plural gaze?

I hear French whispering behind us. I turn and they're beautiful. Tourists, crosshatched with light and shadow, leaning over each other in an overlapping confusion of affection. You sit beside me, preparing in your quiet way for more quietness. It is Maundy Thursday, the front of the program says. I begin Googling *maundy* on my phone but there's no service. I look through the program but find no definition. The sermon is on the exhortation to *Love thy neighbor as thyself*.

How uncanny. This is what I was writing about all morning, revising my dissertation chapter about Toni Morrison's 1987 novel *Beloved* and the idea of the neighbor, as theorized by Christianity, African philosophy, psychoanalysis, and Slavoj Žižek. I turn to tell you this coincidence but the service begins. There is song: the famous boys' choir in tiers, in the same split configuration facing each other. There is sermon. There is standing and sitting. The rustling of programs. Your silhouette out of the corner of my eye. There is the usual meta-desire: a desire for the desire for faith.

Good Friday

THE NEXT DAY, sitting in the upper story of a double decker to the Cambridge train station, I explain my chapter on *Beloved* to you. I'm so entangled in constructing the argument that it takes a while to extricate each of the threads, trace them, and then tie them back together into a coherent tapestry.

Beloved is a mourning for slavery's dismemberment—the literal and figurative tearing apart of both the enslaved's body and community, the Diaspora we invoke so often that we forget its etymological roots in "dispersal." But while the novel brims with a desire to bridge the spaces between a people torn asunder, *Beloved* is also deeply skeptical of union. There is a monstrosity, too, in our longing to be together, which the novel calls "the join" and which many of us would recognize as love.

Beloved was born out of two fragments of history. One was a newspaper story about an enslaved woman, Margaret Garner, who killed her child rather than let her be captured into slavery. The other was a James Van Der Zee photograph of a woman who'd been shot by her lover, but refused to accuse him in the moments before her death. "A woman loved something other than herself so much," Morrison explains in an interview. "She had placed all the value of her life in something outside herself." Love—Sethe's "too thick" love for her children in *Beloved*, the "deepdown, spooky" love between Dorcas and Joe in *Jazz*—is a form of self-displacement. It's as if by allowing something inside of us (a baby, a ghost, a man), we push our selves outside of ourselves.

Beloved's form, I think, counters this parasitic enmeshed love with an ethics of adjacency, a kind of next-to-ness. "He wants to put his story next to hers," Paul D thinks as he tangles fingers with Sethe at the end of the novel. A brief, contingent, tenuous proximity: each person in their proper place, integrity preserved, a certain decorum. This, I believe, is Morrison's ethics of the neighbor.

The bus is full of sunshine. Your face is patient, curious. My mind is weaving with thought. A rushing, tender feeling. By the time we're out on the platform at the Cambridge train station, I feel I've worked something out, rendered to you, in however a halting and temporary fashion, my ideas about the novel. It's strange, given how often I teach, read, and write on *Beloved*, how rarely I speak about loving it. This being with you in language about it is a way to love it at a slant.

We take the train from Cambridge to King's Cross, and somewhere along the way, the strangers—the friends of friends with whom we're traveling—board. We sit across from them and bat words around the otherwise empty train car, a lazy volley of wry, diffident jokes. She is British; he is American. His legs are spread wide; she has made caves of her eyes with kohl. Fluffs of pollen float into the cabin and whip around like snow's sibling. The morning is yellow and blue and green.

Together, we take the Tube from King's Cross to Paddington. Clustered awkwardly at the top of an escalator, we deliberate just long enough to make us almost miss the train we're deliberating about. We race to catch it—a team, a tribe—breathless and charmed by our redundant haste. How spirited the contact between us, how brief! Because in the end, we arrive too early at the small station near the estate we're going to visit. We pass the time by eating lunch. The lull, the mere disparity in what we each choose for our meals, separate us again. We wait in silence for the car to come and fetch us.

The car is dark and unmarked and unmetered. It loops around a tangle of roads. Then out of nowhere, our driver begins to race a white convertible beside us. The drivers open their windows and shout at each other in a wind-riven patois. In the back seat, our upper arms and outer thighs are already touching. Now our glances touch. But none of us says a word. We're still strangers. I smile to myself. This will be a story if we don't die first. The white convertible vanishes at a roundabout. The rest of the ride into the estate is leafy, serpentine, severed by gates. The gravel drive grumbles.

When the car stops in a circular drive, a golden retriever flubbers out of the impressively large and square mansion, our hostess and her boyfriend chasing after it in welcome. The driver hands our bags to us from the boot. Wiping dog-slobbered fingers on our jeans, we step inside. Expensive-looking paintings hang on the walls, without placards—a test of the museum effect?—and distantly visible in a room to the left is a "real Lichtenstein tea set," you whisper to me.

We're guided to our room by our hostess, who is barefoot, in jean shorts. She's just shy of being shy—or seems bored of being shy—about the wealth on display. Her parents are traveling so we have the run of the mansion. There will be no formal dinner. The strangers drop their bags in one wing and we walk the long corridors to ours, enormous windows flashing snippets of green. Our suite is enormous and stuffy. Even the bathroom is carpeted. *Dreams from My Father* sits innocently on a side table. I make a joke to you—or rather, to myself. You'd already started to recede from me on the train. Now you're gone, fully inside whatever fugue of class insecurity this place and these people have conjured for you.

We take a walk—three couples, one dog—across the estate. We cross fields of staring, stalwart cows who menace us with Pavlovian habits, approaching to be milked. We see a man with a camera and a woman with a horse, trespassing miserably. Our hostess tells them off with her soft, authoritative voice and they stumble away to take glamour shots elsewhere. We move through a haze of bluebells. We throw a stick to the dog, who fetches it endlessly, joyously. One of us gets lost and the others hang about and pee behind bushes until we decide he can find his way home. We walk together in sunbaked ruts, between shadowy bushes.

Back at the estate, we take a dip in the heated pool, testing the relative float of beer bottles as we drink them. We use a beloved tennis ball to coax the dog into the water, laughing at his fear and delight. We each touch only our lovers (you barely touch me) and the thought pesters me that in another era, we would all be naked by now, and fucking. We climb up to the roof. We smoke a joint—ah, the comforting surety of chemical effect—and are granted the gift of the giggles and time's spun dilation. Next to me, you are close up and far away at once, as if through a fish eye lens. The setting sun is a discrete circle, clouds peeling jagged rinds around it. It lowers itself into the land and we rise into the colors it leaves behind. The evening is orange and purple and grey.

There's a lasagna the cook has left for us and we heat it up and eat it. I can't taste it, either because I'm stoned or because I'm still sick. I experience only its hot, thick chewiness and a nugatory hunger for more. After dinner, there's some billiards game named after Frieda

Kahlo that involves running in circles and sending the balls catapulting across the table. I opt out, sulking at the insufferable frenzy of these white people. I am so lonely for you. I feel those automatic vibrations that smoking weed always sparks in my skin. I long for you; you are right beside me. We don't have sex that night, though.

Sethe and Beloved are so close, so *joined*, that when one drinks, the other passes water. When Beloved becomes pregnant—inseminated by Paul D—Sethe begins to wither away, emaciating to the point that the skin between her index finger and thumb is thin as paper. Beloved herself is a conjoined being. Morrison's words in interview suggest to me that the character is comprised of two beings who have merged: the baby girl whom Sethe killed with a chainsaw, and an enslaved African woman whom a white man has locked in a box and subjected to torture and rape. The baby girl ghost, banished from the house at 124 Bluestone Road, swims in a stream nearby. The African woman escapes her imprisonment and steps into the water. There they meet and join: "I am loving her face so much   my dark face is close to me   I want to join   she whispers   she chews and swallows me   I am alone   I want to be the two of us   I want the join."

Black Saturday

WE MANAGE TO eke out a morning fuck, toothy but barely fleshed. After, you go for a run, strumming your anxiety into a song for yourself. I lie naked in bed, stretching my feet to reach a migrating splash of sun, and read about Obama's community work in Chicago. When we've showered and dressed, we come down and eat breakfast with the others, trading sections of the newspaper.

Then we three girls lie on a lawn even greener than King's—we're permitted to step on the grass here—chatting while the three boys play with some specialized toy: aeronautic, fluorescent, recursive. We swim again in the pool, which is set into a little mound of a hill. You throw the precious tennis ball over the bushes, and we watch the retriever—named for something Greco-Roman—leap off the edge of the world only to reappear over and over, his tongue flapping around the ball. He's loath to release it every time, torn between the respective blisses of keeping it and getting it. This is the boomerang shape of my desire for you. The difference is that I do not just feel its arc inside of me. I see it, I recognize it. I can even name its shape and metaphorize it. I watch the dog with envy.

That night, we have an argument. We're all out on the patio: wrought iron furniture, curated stones, murky garden statues. We're sitting around a table, talking about the shapes of trees. I give an off-handed compliment to our hostess's boyfriend—his socks are nice, I say, admiring their Easter theme. He thanks me and complains about having to wear boring socks at his office job.

"You can at least enjoy color on your toes, no?"

"No," says the third man, the stranger from the train, whose own family wealth back in Maine, you've told me, has an extra burden of concealment, the bluff of gruffness. He understands, the gentleman from Maine says now, why businessmen find it necessary to be professional, and he too believes socks should be discreet—no bright colors, no patterns.

He cannot defend this position, however, when pressed. He cannot prove that there's anything quintessentially professional about boring socks, that they index anything real about doing your job well. I am, of course, the one who presses him. You roll your eyes but I can't tell why.

"The point is not that I am an artsy-fartsy dilettante," I fume, "the point is that I *am* professional, and that my socks—and my clothes—have nothing to do with it."

But I've already proved his point by going on about it so hysterically, by rejecting the terms of his stuffy pragmatism. Oh, silly, colorful me!

Easter Sunday

I SNIFFLE QUIETLY in the jolting taxi van we take back to the station. When we get there, we hug the other couple with polite, false promises. We run in pairs to catch our respective trains and wave goodbye from afar, on tiptoes, smiling. Once we're alone, I apologize to you at length for all the terrible things I'm sure I said unconsciously about rich people and white people. Habit, I plead. You dismiss the apology, say it's unnecessary and disingenuous, which is true and makes it worse.

On the train to Bristol, we settle into our parallel grooves again. While you doze, I look out the window. How many windows have I stared out of with this choke in my throat? As we near the station, I start to feel guilty for having forgotten Easter presents and the names of my cousin's children. I buy some chocolate eggs at the station kiosk and instruct you to ask subtly after their names. You botch it slightly but your stilted question receives a sprightly reply, with an alliterative mnemonic even. My cousin is lovely, as brisk as my aunt but warmer, if that isn't just the fallacy of phrenology talking: her face is rounder than her mother's, her cheeks duskier, her eyes bluer.

We go for a walk in the woods—the whole family, two dogs, you and me. My lilac flats somehow stay pristine. We chat about whether different dog breeds perceive each other as distinct races or other species. There is a famous bridge and some photos. You and I both have the cold now. We sniff and cough through the loose, rambling dinner—couscous and kebabs—at the wooden kitchen table, indulging the children's quirks. I notice how my cousin bites her nails when we talk about school—she is back doing an MA in English—and that she and one daughter are caught up in a cycle of annoyance and assurance, snapping at each other, then covering it over with concerted fondness. The proximity of the jabs and the strokes makes everything seem bantering and loving.

Maybe this backdrop is what makes the thing stand out so much. They've bought a summer house in France that they rent out, but only to donate the money to charity. What for? I wonder. It feels unheard of to use property this way, especially for an atheist family for whom Easter seems mostly to entail a joking battle over chocolate and its consequences. They seem surprised by my surprise. Raising their children right obviously means being charitable. Nothing to do with religion at all.

Over dessert, my cousin and I revel in similarities and differences—we laugh at our parents' foibles and shake our heads at our own. Her eldest daughter gazes at me over her plate. She may just be a dreamy girl—just like my brother's middle child, we speculate in our mania for comparison—but I want to think my singularity compels her: a brown woman with short hair, always in bright colors, traveling with her much younger American boyfriend. Does it disappoint her that I'm paired off with you? Does she judge the hunger in my eyes when you leave the room? Or am I judging myself through her eyes? How to stop dissolving into you. How to stop succumbing to solitude. How to love without swallowing you. I gaze back at her. I wish I could be her age while being my age at the same time: subject to love's rampage but knowingly so. A lens that zooms out while zooming in.

Baby Suggs has discernment. She knows when enough is enough. She knows that when Sethe kisses her children, she kisses them too much. She recoils when Sethe tries to feed one baby breast milk while still soaked in the blood of the one she's just killed. There is such a thing as a too-much touch. To grasp someone is sometimes to choke them. But Baby Suggs knows how to touch. When Sethe arrives back in their town, she is torn up, by childbirth and pregnancy, by being a fugitive, and by an outrageous whipping when she was enslaved, so forceful the scars are like "a tree on my back." Baby Suggs' touch soothes Sethe. Baby Suggs heals Sethe's body by cleaning one part of it at a time.

I long for a touch that is discerning like this, two-sided, delicate. Is it foolish to aspire to the state of skin itself? We sleep separately that night—in a narrow wooden bed and a springy metal cot—too sick to bother with the teenagey squeeze of spooning in one. Our pattern is not easy to throw off.

Easter Monday

I WAKE FEELING tangled and low. Neither of us slept well because of the cold we're passing back and forth. We both nap on the train back to Cambridge and are quiet on the bus home. You shower and head straight to the lab. I email you a couple of hours later with some hybrid plea: an ultimatum plus a guilt trip plus an apology. "Maybe we should just live in parallel like you want and not joined together like I want," I write. I almost mean it. I try to work on my *Beloved* chapter. I heat up Sainsbury's soup for lunch. I can't taste it and it burns my tongue and my eyes brim with self-pity.

In the afternoon, I flee the barren desk, the blank, wheezing laptop on top of it, and put on a coat and walk to Jesus Green. A gray day, an empty park. I trace the stream that curlicues along its furthest end. I have an hour until *Source Code* starts at the Vue Cinema, a twenty-minute walk from here. Ducks yell and snort, the bespoke gentlemen bullying the fuzzy ladies. I follow them, move at a duck's pace for a while. A mother wobbles along the bank, then slides into the stream, a flustery swarm as her chicks follow. They form a jerky arrow, mother's beak the point. Abruptly, she darts and her babies swirl and bob in confusion as she pecks at some floating thing. I think it's rubbish but when I draw closer, I see it's a dead baby duck. Is she trying to eat it or wake it? Horror.

When the ducks slip around a bend in the river, I exit Jesus Green through a stately arch of chestnut trees. Tracking my way to the cinema on Google Maps, I glance up and see a spire, one I've admired before for its pleasing thinness. As I approach, I see a sign outside: "Historic Church Open." I read another sign about who made it and when, and who fixed it up and when. I decide to go in—why not?— more in the name of tourism than religion. That meta-desire to believe. I have to admit to myself that I've had this urge many times in the past few years, whenever I am out walking and see a church: to walk in and sit and not pray, exactly, but think about prayer.

As I finger the guestbook, I notice a woman of about my mother's age and skin tone sitting in the last pew. She's wearing a pink plaid wool coat and she's crying. She turns, sees me, stops briefly; then sniffs and resumes her passionate weeping. She's almost choking with it. I don't sign my name in the guestbook. I walk to the front of the church, staying out of her way, staring at my lilac shoes in quiet dismay. I look around at the stained glass. I stare at the altar. I sit in the front pew and wait. After five minutes of deliberating in the sob-racked silence, I decide that I should try to help.

I walk back to her pew.

"Are you okay?"

She shakes her head.

"Can I help?"

She nods.

I sit next to her and put my hand on her back. "What's wrong?" I ask. And she tells me.

She's a student of the ministry and lives with her children in a seminary across the street. But the church hasn't let her proceed with her coursework since September and she has been excluded from all parish activities. After a pause, I ask why. Well, back when she was living in London, she'd been "attacked" by her neighbors. She reported them. But someone made "further allegations"—"fair enough," she says cryptically—and now she's waiting for the main office in London to determine whether she'll be permitted to proceed. Her superiors here have started interrogating her: Why did she leave her country twenty years ago? How does she feel about becoming a British citizen? She wants to end her life, she says, because "once the church has rejected you, you have nothing left."

She cries through the entire story. Her face is like a rocky brown waterfall; her hair is dyed maroon and droops over it like lichen. I coo and rub her back, my hand warming as it chafes against her coat. When silence yawns, I speak. I tell this woman that she's in the right, everyone else in the wrong. I tell her she should start her life anew here in Cambridge, for her children's sake. Like her, I have a green passport; unlike her, I have a right-of-abode stamp inside it, thanks to my British-born father. Yet I preach to this woman all the actions that we both know very well she cannot take.

Guiltily, I look around. God. He's right there, within reach, all around us, in the very wooden walls faintly giving us back our voices. And so, stumbling a little, I begin to speak of God—as if I know anything of God—I say that God loves her, that God is with her and for her, that every good act she has ever committed is because of His faith in her. The word God is a heavy coin on my tongue. What I really want to say is: *Find a fucking job! You have kids!* Instead I speak of God, how He knows she has done nothing wrong, how He would want her to care for her children.

In the midst of this mesmeric Godspeak, the two of us swaying, an older white man and woman come into the church. They walk right past to the front, ignoring us entirely. She whispers to me. They know her, they live and work at her ministry center, the way they shunned her just now is how it is all the time. I look at her, then at them, back at her. She sobs.

"What country are you from?" I ask.

"Why?" Her eyes swivel warily toward me. But before I can soften my question or prevaricate, she replies: "Zimbabwe."

I gasp happily, inappropriately. "I'm from Zambia!"

She shrugs, eyes damp. She doesn't care that our countries are neighbors. England is her country, isn't that what she's been telling the Church, telling me, this whole time? She rambles, her name tumbling out in the slurry of words. She does not ask mine. Eventually, she thanks me, apologizes for keeping me, and says I should go. I stand, my hand on her shoulder.

I tell her, in parting, that God loves her, that God wants her to be strong. The words are thick as thieves in my mouth. As if I know anything of strong, I who am so weak for you, you who are so weak for power and wealth and the approval of strangers. As if I know anything of God, God who is a gentle thought for which I wish I could wish.

You ring my cell phone just as I'm leaving the church and we decide to meet up to watch the movie together. Our way of making up is to sit beside each other in the dark facing a giant screen. Out of the corner of my eye, I glance at your profile—sharp-nosed and pale in the glowing blue black—and feel stupidly elated by your nearness. I touch your hand and you let me. It's almost enough, to put my story next to yours. But *Source Code* leaves me antsy, unsettled. Time travel movies always do.

FIVE WAYS TO EAT TERMITES

Anna Andrew

Dedicated to the South Sudanese refugee women in Cairo whose experiences and struggles inspired this story.

ONE: EAT THE termites raw.

Two: Fry them with a little salt but no oil because termites are a fatty insect.

Three: Boil them, and let them dry on the sand, then grind them into a paste the consistency of peanut butter, then eat them with bread if you have any.

Four: Crush raw termites into a ball and fry, like meatballs, to add to soup.

Five: Boil water, add salt and add three or four handfuls of raw termites, then stir until you have a thick, white soup.

1968. THE REGIONS of southern Sudan, now an independent country called South Sudan, were ravaged by war. The southern Sudanese refugees in Uganda were hungry. We were starving and we were broke. We didn't know what money looked like, let alone what it was or the kind of real difference it could make. I was born in 1962 and I never saw money until I was ten. What we had was a grass hut that a friend of my grandfather's gave us when we were thrown into the Ugandan jungle in 1964 to escape the militia that ransacked our village. We didn't have clothes. We fled to Uganda half-naked, finding discarded sacks that used to hold bundles of cotton, and tying them around our waists. But the pressing need, that weighed on us every waking minute of our lives, was food.

Hungry, it's pretty impossible to be happy. You feel you are not a part of the world. Hunger is its own kind of exile. But we had to survive. We had to eat. The question is what? Our first year in Uganda, my mother weeded millet fields, from sunrise to sundown, day in day out. As compensation, the farmers gave her two cups of millet or sorghum, or one piece of cassava. My sister and brothers and I would wait impatiently for her to come and grind the millet she'd gotten into flour and boil it with water into a paste—what we called pudding.

Lokung had no rivers so there was no fish, really, only streams made by rain. I was seven years old. We were originally from Magwi, Eastern Equatoria, and in 1964, the Northern militia, called the Adjana, raided our village. They caught my father. My sister and two brothers and my mother and I ran to the jungle. I was two going on three years old and my older brother carried me on his neck. We took refuge in a grass hut in the village of Lokung, owned by my grandfather's friend. There was no money, I didn't even see coins or notes until I was about ten years old.

In the Mango season, March to May, no one is hungry. There are mangos. We picked wild vegetables in the forest. Green pea-leaves, we grew at home. And carcadia-leaves, and other summer leaves, too. Ongubi we boiled and ate with okra. Jakajaka and kibui and alaktar, green peas that grow wild in the forest and in the summer blossom into a beautiful white flower, we boiled as well and ate with peanut butter or sesame paste.

In the market they sold fruits, bananas and oranges, but we had no money. Cow meat was expensive, two Ugandan schillings per kilo. Finagling two shillings is impossible. You work for sorghum or millet.

In Uganda the place we stayed at was on the border. We stayed there about half a year and my father still was not there. It was taking too long to wait for my father to be brought to us and we left the border.

Anyanya, the rebel movement fighting the Northern government and its raiding militias, trying to recruit men to join its ranks, came one evening. My mother was grinding millet. We heard the sounds of shooting, now familiar though no less frightening, and my mother said get up, get up, tried to grab us to go, but it was too late. Our home was already full of soldiers. They took her away. My older brother picked up the bundle that was our baby sister and we scurried in the dark into the bush. They took her and others to carry plundered food and crates of ammunition. The next day our mother came back. They'd released her after seeing that her breasts were dripping milk.

The Ugandan army came with two tanks. We were gathered from the bush. They said we needed to go to a safe place. We crossed the border into Uganda on foot.

The food here was different. In southern Sudan we had chicken and cow meat and fish, plenty of fish fresh from the Nile, that we dried to preserve and then boiled to make soup with peanut butter or sesame paste. Fried onions with oil and tomatoes and okra, that was my favorite dish. Boiled hibiscus leaves with dry fish, stirred in peanut butter and served with sweet potatoes, that was our family's regular meal. My mother was a good cook.

We changed. We ate different food. We were not used to eating leaves except black pea leaves. A different food is a different home. We were not home.

1969–1971 THERE was peace. I had many Ugandan friends, mostly from school. Uganda had its own problems, though not as violent as back home. During Christmas the religious divide between Protestants and Catholics was very visible. But it was still peaceful. A peaceful decade for us.

My mother worked in the field all day. We worked in the house, cleaning and cooking. My mother told me what to do when she wasn't home. My sister and I would trade chores of cleaning and cooking. Peaceful years. Even my younger brother learned to cook, by watching us.

In the dry season we ate turtle. It tasted like chicken. My grandfather liked to eat wild things. I was only three years old, but I remember. He fought in the Second World War. He was a soldier in the jungle with the rebels, and soldiers eat wild things. Soldiers are wild men. My grandfather knew Idi Amin, fought alongside him, when he was young.

He was a raw man, my grandfather, and liked to eat things raw. Raw okra. Raw maize. Pick and eat. That was his style of eating, this man! He liked me very much. He told me tales about his soldiering. He started in Juba, fighting Gondokoro, later his battalion moved to Mangalla. we'd walk from Mangalla to Torit on foot, he would tell me. I married with my own money, he'd boast, the money I made on my feet. My grandmother married my mother to his son. He paid the bride-wealth. He caught turtles and cooked them himself. He will put the pot on the fire and make his own food. Anna! Come and eat! My grandmother hated turtle. She is a clean woman. But she loves termites, she knows how to make them very good.

Elephant meat. Very hard to kill an elephant but the meat is good. Women are not supposed to eat it. My mother and grandmother they'd say it's not a woman's meat. Very nice, red-black, you dry it on the fire. After cutting it into cubes, I'd boil it for a long time and then cook it. If you have some peanut butter to go with it, that's amazing, but salt is enough. Salt, water and meat, that's all you need to make an elephant dish to die for. We had to cook it outside. My mother did not eat it, being a woman. I was probably the only woman to taste elephant meat. We couldn't even use the dishes in the house. We had special dishes for elephant meat.

1983. THE WAR returned. No food, all roads closed. My mother could no longer get millet. We had returned to Juba, lived in the middle of the city. It went on for more than a decade, the war, and it was bad. By 2000 things were awful, the war was still raging on. Everyone was trying to farm, sporadically because of the constant bombing and raiding. Many died of starvation. Even I, still young, planted some sorghums, but very little grew, you could not live on it for a year.

Our family moved to Khartoum in 2001.

Khartoum. Very bad, the worst. I had to brew alcohol. The ingredients are simple: dates, sugar and yeast. It would take three days to distill it. You put the dates, soaked in water in a container on fire. You need a bowl and two saucepans, one with holes. When the dates drips into the bowl in the other saucepan, tied over with cloth, what comes out is alcohol. You bottle it and sell. Date liquor sells for five Sudanese pounds. Muslims, who have money in Khartoum, are the best costumers, even though it's haram. If you are caught by the moral police, they take everything and fine you 1,000 Sudanese pounds. Otherwise you rot in jail. But we found ways to hide the crime: you dig a hole, away from your home, and bury the alcohol there in the ground.

Brewing alcohol, it must be done at night, quietly. Neighbors cannot hear, some neighbors are bad. Sometimes police go house to house, and they generally suspect the Nubians and southern Sudanese war-displaced populations scattered in camps outside the city. If you go to the Omdurman Jail, you see majority of the inmates are southern Sudanese and Nubians, both Christian and Muslim, many in there for petty offenses and others for political reasons.

It was only for money, brewing alcohol. I never drank it. I made it to pay my way to Cairo.

CATCHING TERMITES. YOU find a small hill and make two holes at the bottom of the hill and put leaves around it like a hat, so the termites can't go up. They go down and they all come into the hole and when the hole is full, in about half an hour, you scoop them up and put them in cotton bags. We can eat for three months what I catch in a day. We boil them so they don't go bad. We clean the wings—we don't eat them. They're like wax. Eat the flesh only.

And bushrat, too, we ate. My brother caught one and we cooked it. He brought it home. We boiled water and put the whole body in, then took the fur off. You can eat it plain, very delicious. If you have peanut butter or sesame paste, prepare it that way. If you want it dry, you put it under the fire in an oven. So delicious.

MY SIBLINGS:
    Two born in Uganda.
    Four more in Sudan.
    We were ten children, four died.

sound modeling

Anca Roncea

tied to the land there is no language. there is sound tied to
this language. there is no language after this. this is the
language that was given to us

behind the glass of this car the world purrs shut-off gentle.
there is no other we are attached to the other you can't trust
your own cells there are hunts in our dreams

who we were before 1989 was buried under the
noncommunicated and the uncommunicable this is supposed
to feel heavy. sometimes speaking simultaneously there are
silences rewriting history. 1984 had already occurred

I was taught to knit when I was 9. Antigone defied the system
in favor of the uncommunicable process of mourning and
closure. Our country has a lacuna, our mourning spills
through our pores

her stories were her stubbornness her generation is dying is
alcohol and impossible longing the phone fills up with our
torn intimacy why were we expected to empty as if we would
become cosmugglers

sensible sensitive fragile songlike ultraprecise seismograph.
linden trees insensitive to urgent echoes carve out a space in
Romanian. we walked in the mist with hands of vetiver
bergamot and petitgrain

every time we were on the phone and the line crackled we
knew we were listened to by them. in them lines of memory
and banishment.

RED CURRANTS

Catharina Coenen

Q: I couldn't resist picking up some truly beautiful red currants at the farmer's market this morning even though I have no idea what to do with them. Any suggestions? —Sent by Katie
http://www.thekitchn.com/what-can-i-do-with-red-currant-121190

SOMETIMES RED CURRANTS at the farmer's market glow like dashboard warning lights, the sugar in my shopping basket drags on my arm like lead, and sweetness, beauty, danger taste the same. Sometimes my eyes project the letters from a sign outside the Licht- und Luftbad in Essen, Germany, onto the walls of a new world. Sometimes my retina and taste buds feel like my grandmother's, rather than my own. I cannot tell the currant story in third person, because, though she lived and told it, it is mine.

THE WOMAN STOPS in mid-greeting and mid-step; I nearly bash her knees with the picnic basket swinging from my hand.

"What's wrong?" I ask, balancing the basket on my forearm to rummage through blanket, coffee flask, fork, spoon, making sure the bag of sugar is still wedged upright, between the currants and the white enamel bowl. She doesn't answer, doesn't move. I look up from the basket, then further up at her face. She gazes past me; I turn to trace the line of her fixed stare. The entrance lodge to the Licht- und Luftbad looks the same as always: red geraniums, peeling paint, tack-bitten wood around the ticket booth window cluttered with signs—women this way, men that way, admissions prices, rules and regulations, opening times. Even the porter is the same.

"What is it?" I ask.

Sweat trickles down my neck. My head feels addled, as though in sudden supplication to this fifty-sixth day of unrelenting heat. I gaze back at her. Shadows bloom across her face, her eyes expressionless beneath black bangs, the skin across her cheek bones blanched under its summer tan. She shifts her weight and gives a little shake, as if to rouse herself.

"I can't go in."

It takes another minute, too many seconds, for my eyes to swivel between the entrance booth and her face. Too much time for a thought to drop.

"Oh."

She turns, slowly, away from the entrance. Away from the sign. My delight to see her here, again, today fades to confusion. My brain flicks through images, in search of sense: A deluge of air- and light-filled afternoons. The woman's slender shape in the sunbather's dress, long arms flying skyward, her fist hitting the ball dead-center. The sparkle in her eyes as she turns to her team, punches the air: "There, we've shown them!" The hours—how many?—of rest in grassy shade, my picnic blanket spread in sight of hers. Stolen glances, in between the fork's glide along pale-green stems. My eyes detach from red orbs pinging into the enamel bowl, touch eyelids, trace lashes, the curves of her arms and chest, the wild flood of her hair. Each de-stemmed currant's single drop of red in a white-crystal bed, hurried spoon-scratch—I scramble to my feet to follow her into another round of ball, leaving berries to bleed into their sugar coats. Returned to the blanket, breathless from play, I spoon and chew as, three paces away, her graceful gestures straighten her dress, re-pin her hair. Inside my mouth, coated pearls explode acid, gritty crunch of half-dissolved sweet, grain-pulp of seeds and skins.

Since days grew hot in June, I have hauled a pound of currants through each sun-soaked afternoon, my sandals plopping across sidewalk pavers awash in broiling heat, twenty minutes from the corner grocery by my parents' rental flat, down block after block of workers' housing, to this green oasis. After days of gloom and dust, selling cigarettes, three at a time, to men and boys who can't find work, this is where I come to breathe, to laugh, to be at ease in women's company. The Licht- und Luftbad is my refuge, my place away from home, from town, from voices on the radio.

The basket drags against my arm, imprinting red streaks of braided willow onto skin.

"Then I'm not going in either," I say, seeking her eyes. She nods, once, then turns away. Tears sting. I blink through blurs. I do not need to read the bold-faced print, the words, not meant for me, already too ubiquitous for me to see. Two lines, four words. JEWS NOT WELCOME HERE.

MY OMA LOTTE told this story again and again. Currants brought it on. Reminiscences of hot summers. Deliberations on the merits and dangers of sunbathing, discussions of the value of ball sports for girls. Each time her Jewish friend's beauty bundles the story's light. Never a name, never an indication that the two of them talked more than to acknowledge each other in greeting. Each time the shock at connecting the sign to a face, the instant decision not to go in: a burnt fuse, a breaker switch thrown, lights-out.

Red currants glow inside a basket. A white sign on brown wood. Black letters slap a label on black curls. My grandmother stood, stunned. She turned and left. She did not return. Then, she got pregnant.

Less than six months after this last visit to the Licht- und Luftbad, unmarried, still living with her parents, and without the financial wherewithal to start a household, my grandmother, Sophie Charlotte Philippine Weber, conceived my aunt Elfriede, her first child. Lotte hadn't just met my grandfather, Alfred; they didn't make a baby in a star-struck burst of pheromonal fog. Alfred had been part of her group of male friends for many years. Her mother, Sophie, habitually snapped back at Philippine and Charlotte, my grandmother's two busy-body aunts, that, as long as Lotte was hanging out with boys by the dozen, there was no room for hanky-panky. Great-grandma Sophie was correct—by mid-December of 1936 Lotte had been dancing and flirting with these men for many years. She wasn't stupid, inexperienced, or seventeen—she was an adult woman, nearly twenty-five years of age.

And certainly, it wasn't that she didn't know where babies come from—she was well aware. Of all her male friends she most enjoyed evenings-out with one, whom she described as ein Süßer—a "sweet man," meaning he was gay. With him, she felt relaxed, because she didn't need a plan for when and how to say "no." They just had fun together, at concerts, dancing, hiking, talking about books and films. Until the day he was gone. Abgeholt—"taken away," the code word for being picked up by the Gestapo or SS.

I regret that I don't know his name. I think she may have said—and I forgot. Willi, perhaps, or Heinrich, or Karl. I do remember he had brothers, parents, a close-knit family who cared. I don't know how old I was when she first mentioned him—old enough to know what that meant: abgeholt. Past my first history lesson on the Third Reich. At least in the third grade. Old enough, for sure, to remember a name, or to ask: "How did you find out? What did his parents do?" To ask: "What did you think?" To ask: "Were you scared?"

I never asked. I listened, but I don't remember asking anything. I listened to her stories of currants and of her friends as I had listened to her telling me about Lilly, the angel—naptime tales of a grandmother's imagination. I knew Lilly, though she had a name, was invented; the Jewish woman, nameless, was real; the gay friend was real. I listened the same, no matter whom she was talking about—enthralled, as though listening to music. Not talking back, not asking. Just taking the words that came my way, tucking them in, out of sight—each gleaming splinter wrapped, with care, into folds of a child's soft and winding brain.

MANY YEARS AGO, in the vibration-free basement of a northern German university, I took a class on using the electron microscope. To thin-slice plant tissues for its high-resolving beam, I made knives by breaking blocks of glass, creating blades much sharper than steel but also much more delicate. I was taught never to touch the cutting edge, that putting your finger there not only slices skin but blunts the blade, renders it useless. I cannot know what my grandmother's story-fragments meant to her, how they fit together, what shape they made within her thoughts, her memory, her life. What were these glassy shards? A vase, a mirror, a window, a drinking glass? Did the encounter by the porter's lodge really happen when I imagine it did, before my grandmother was married? How long before that did her gay friend disappear?

The summer in the city of Essen was unusually warm in 1935, unbearably hot in 1936. In all of Germany, Jewish people were banned from public swimming pools in 1935. But the Licht- und Luftbad was not a pool, just a walled-in green space with two partitions, split by sex, where people played on the grass and rested under trees. Its counter-part in Frankfurt-Niederrad, the only one for which I could find records, claims it was the last one to close to Jews, in May of 1938. So: No later than the summer of 1937 for the currants. Not before 1935. Most probably July or August of 1936.

Now, which pile of shards for my grandmother's gay friend? Twenty-six thousand men were imprisoned by Nazi police for "punishable incidents between men," over one hundred thousand were questioned, brutally; thousands found themselves outside of the legal process entirely, in concentration camps. The law to make this possible passed in 1935, but seventy-eight thousand arrests happened within a span of only thirty months: early 1937 to mid-1939. The friend might have vanished right before my grandmother got pregnant. Or right after. Either way, the threat of annihilation was there, imminent, pervasive. Police and storm troops closed gay bars for both men and women in February of 1933; in 1934 the Gestapo sent telegrams to local police ordering lists of men with "known homosexual activity" to be mailed to Berlin. In 1936 the criminal police became part of the Gestapo under Heinrich Himmler, who had been running Hitler's concentration camps since 1934. That year, many gay men and women married, some emigrated, some committed suicide. By the time my grandmother got pregnant, the knowledge that something could happen to her friend hung in the air like poisonous, sticky fog. Perhaps he was already gone.

DESPITE HER RAPT descriptions of her Jewish friend's beauty, I don't believe my grandmother considered that she might be sexually attracted to women. But if she thought about this, would I know? And, more vexing still: Would she have known to label her attraction as anything? Was love between women even talked about? As a teen I knew about gay men—the neighbor who regularly came to my parents' store to tell my mother about his aging partner's cancer and his grief. But women living together flew under the radar, were assumed to be cousins, sisters, friends.

Along with word-fragments, expressions, anecdotes, my memories caught my Oma Lotte's tone of voice. I can still hear her swooning over female lawyers, chief secretaries, doctors, authors, and, once, a baroness: "Eine tolle Frau." The German adjective toll lives on tonality. English dictionaries toss up "neat," but "neat" conveys some distance, a judgment that separates the speaker from the spoken-about. Toll, in German, is unrelated to the English: it knee-buckles in admiration, waves a lighter at the concert, dances in the streets with joy. It is forever star-struck, drunk on hormones, twelve.

MY GRANDMOTHER LOVED my grandfather. My grandparents accomplished more than a lasting marriage, more than mutual care, more than raising three children in terrible, frightening times: Through thirty-four years of marriage, they talked. I know because I heard them speak to each other. I know because my mother heard them, too. I know because, later, my grandmother talked about how they talked. And I know because I have some of my grandfather's letters, sent from the Russian front—letters about the two of them, brimfull of emotion: love, and longing. Anger, homesickness, and fear, humor, care, jealousy, grief, pain, and returning, over and over, to love. Their marriage didn't skirt emotion—they lived it.

Why, then, do my fingers on the keyboard keep tripping into acid-sugar, currant-red, into my grandmother's sandals on hot pavement stones? What makes her story mine to feel, to tell?

Maybe it is mine because she ached to write and never did. Maybe it's mine because I was there, with her, listening. Listening after my grandfather's death, listening when my aunt Elfriede's mind bounced between heaven and hell, listening when my uncle and my mother were so intent on building safe and ordinary lives that, each time my grandmother began to speak about the war, both of them jumped up to do something else, something very urgent that needed to be done exactly then—my uncle, usually, to strum his guitar, my mother to make more coffee.

This story is mine to write because I stayed at the coffee table. It is mine because of shared hours of folding sheets and towels, of stripping currants for jam or cake. It is mine because she told me, because it stuck with me. Maybe I listened differently from everybody else. Maybe what I heard was not my grandmother's story but my own.

MY HUSBAND AND I met in graduate school, en route to a seminar about the genetics of wild sunflowers. That's my story. He says the seminar was about butterflies.

After several failed relationships with men, I was attempting to live happily on my own in a tiny studio apartment plastered onto the side of the oldest house in a small town in Oregon. Both the house and I were transplants: the house from its original site by the Willamette River, I from Northern Germany. Inside its walls, I lit tea lights, rolled out my yoga mat, worked hard towards solitary contentment. But every Wednesday night, on my drive home from a shift at the local food co-op, I cried. I told myself I was just tired.

Hummingbirds buzzed by my new apartment, on their way to the neighbors' *Ribes sanguineum*, Oregon's native currant bush. Forget-me-nots grew around its wooden stoop. Because of the butterflies, it soon also had two people living on 250 square feet. A botany professor called our arrangement "a grafting experiment," tissues forced to fuse by proximity. We easily agreed on taking turns standing to dress or cook and sitting on the bed. After I defended my PhD and before my visa expired, we married, so that we could both live in Germany. Nearly twenty years later, I fell in love with a woman.

Breaking up my marriage felt like untangling grafted hearts—

life-threatening surgery, the hardest thing I ever did. We grieved. We stayed friends. My mother said she hadn't wanted to mention it before, but it had bothered her from the beginning that my wedding picture shows my hand balled in a fist. My husband's smile is rapt, and I smile in return. But my fingers obey a different line of emotional control. After we separated, he cried about the fist. I had noticed it when the pictures came back from the developer. But the part of my brain that saw such things had a habit of fainting into the next armchair instead of making itself heard. Maybe it didn't know what to say or how to say it. Most likely another force within my psyche kept it choked. Until I tried to write about my grandmother eating red currants at the Licht- und Luftbad in 1936, about the disappearance of her gay and Jewish friends, I did not understand that the choking part might be a safety-switch.

THE YEAR BEFORE I moved to Oregon, its voters passed Ballot Measure 8, which repealed the governor's regulations to shield gay people from discrimination. The repeal enabled landlords to evict tenants based on sexual orientation and employers to fire them. I first heard about Measure 8 in 1992, when the Oregon Citizens Alliance put forth ballot Measure 9, which declared homosexuality to be "abnormal, wrong, unnatural and perverse" and demanded that schools, public universities, and all government branches expel gay employees.

After the election I walked around in shock. It felt physical, a slug to the gut, an intensity I couldn't label or explain. My co-workers pointed out that there was no reason to be dismayed: the ballot measure had been defeated after all. Fifty-six percent "against" was a resounding victory, they said. But I could not stop counting off strangers in the street, wondering who had voted "in favor." Forty-three percent, to me, looked very much like "nearly half"—just about every other person. My stomach tightened, yet my head told soothing stories of how my belly-clench horror was sympathetic, someone else's, the threat of expulsion never about me.

Two years later, Measure 13, banning books by or about gay people from public libraries, failed even more narrowly, by a little under

19,000 votes. A fellow graduate student and her girlfriend spent a night in a protest camp on campus, just around the corner from where we worked in our labs. Someone took pot shots at their tent. I felt outraged. And shaky. And still, I told myself my rage and fear were only about threats to favourite books and to my friends.

Over the following years, I saw three doctors for inexplicable exhaustion, brain fog, stomach and kidney troubles. My diaries of this time despair over all-encompassing fatigue, vague pains, and inconclusive medical exams, but never once mention the election. Instead, pages and pages about feeling safe inside my relationship alternate with desperation over not wanting sex. Never once a sentence about feeling attracted to women, and no memories of such thoughts. But there, on an empty page, à propos of nothing, a newspaper clipping, a grainy black-and-white photograph of a painting by Hans von Aachen from 1604: Die drei Grazien—three standing nude women, a triangle of interlocking arms, arranged to display breasts, thighs, bellies, buttocks from the front, the back, the side.

WOMEN DON'T NEED a grandmother who came of age in a fascist state to be blind-sided by a first same-sex attraction in mid-life. There are books about this, scientific studies, online discussion groups. Some hypothesize that late-onset changes in sexual orientation arise from hormonal change. Some propose that being attracted to one sex for part of our life and another at another time is part of sexual fluidity, that this is how humans are made, and that only culture induces us to think otherwise. One of my friends claims that all women are sexually drawn to other women, but that few of us dare to live that attraction.

I thought women being more attractive than men was just how things were, objectively. I remember a moment on a college trip: a shared bathroom, glancing into a large mirror over a row of sinks. Behind me, a curvy fellow student stands naked, the perfect renaissance nude. She waves her hands, raves about a man she met. "Wow," I thought. "I can really see what that guy must see in her." Yet, that was it. I don't remember thinking about touching, about anything beyond the pleasure of this stolen glance.

My MOTHER SAYS my grandmother kept secrets. A day or two after I tell her that I've fallen in love with a woman, she calls me on the phone.

"I've remembered something," she says. "After the war, your Oma Lotte used to take me and Elfriede to see two of her friends. We called them "aunts," but they weren't really related to us or to each other. They lived in Essen, so we would sometimes take the train to see them when your grandfather was out of town."

Images of a trip with my grandmother rise in my mind. "Did they live in a very small apartment?" I ask. "In one of those giant apartment blocks with a lawn in the center? Was there a bathtub in their kitchen, with a board on top, so that it worked like a kind of counter?"

"Yes," my mother says. "Yes, that's how it was. And whenever she took us, she said we absolutely could not tell your grandfather where we had been."

"What do you mean?" I ask.

"It was because your grandfather was very jealous," my mother says. "I now wonder if those two women were a couple. I know your Oma Lotte was fiercely fond of them. And your grandfather would get really angry when she mentioned them. Each time we went there, she was adamant that we could not tell him that we had gone to see them. "

My mother's mention of my grandfather's jealousy sounds familiar. I look back through my transcripts of Opa Alfred's letters from the Russian front. Because Lotte decided that her children did not need to know everything about their parents' marriage, she culled much of what he wrote. But some of his surviving letters bounce from cursing his own jealousy into angry admonishments that my grandmother spent too much time in conversations with other women instead of writing to him about more details of her daily life. Some letters reference other—missing—letters, drawn-out written fights.

Later, I remember that Oma took my sister and me to see the "aunts" after my grandfather had passed away, when I was maybe ten. When I ask my sister about her memories from that trip, she describes being fascinated by a photograph in their apartment, showing one of the women in a fancy dress and swooping hat: young, beautiful, glamorous—an actress, my sister thought.

Was there one bedroom in that no-room-to-turn-around apartment? Were there two? Who were my grandmother's women friends? What were they to each other and to her? All I know is that the very moment I told my mother that I had fallen in love with a female friend, the forbidden childhood visits to the "aunties" rose immediately in her mind.

UNLIKE GAY MEN, women in Nazi Germany were not usually locked up or killed for same-sex relations. The unspoken assumption was that they could be forced to marry and would still give birth to babies for the Führer's war. As long as they kept silent and played along, they survived.

Change was slow to come. In 1957, the German supreme court ruled that paragraph 175 of German criminal law, which forbade same-sex relations, was "insufficiently related to Nazi law" to necessitate a reconsideration. This ruling kept same-sex relationships illegal until 1969, by which time fifty thousand men had been sentenced in court. The criminal police continued to maintain "pink lists" of gay men until 1978. Through my early adolescence, love between women remained implicitly illegal—as safe as it was invisible. Marriage between same-sex partners only became legal in Germany two years ago.

CURRANTS AND LOVE survive by local law. Few Americans know the taste of currants, fewer yet crave it as a taste of home. In Pennsylvania, where I now live, currants are hard to find, because currant bushes were out-lawed in 1933. Several states had already banned planting of any members of the genus *Ribes* in the early 1900s to prevent a tree disease called White Pine Blister Rust. Because most modern currant cultivars carry resistance genes to the rust fungus, Pennsylvania no longer enforces its ban. When neighbors gave me extra currant bushes from their yards, I crossed my fingers that no one would care to resurrect old prohibitions and planted joy in glowing red. Each summer, robins, chickadees and cardinals beat me to the harvest, but every remaining berry spills childhood memories inside my mouth.

My sister once walked by the Licht- und Luftbad on a trip with my Oma Lotte, when they went to find the house where Oma grew up. Deep in the workers' quarters of Essen, close to Krupp's steel factory, they trudged through streets lined with apartment buildings, each block of houses a square shaped around a central lawn, green space originally designed for spreading laundry to bleach in the sun, now turned into playgrounds.

I ask my sister whether they met with any of Oma Lotte's friends while they were there.

"No," my sister says, "remember, she was the only one who got away."

I frown: "Away from what?"

My sister says the Licht- und Luftbad was where my grandmother met her commie friends.

"Her commie friends?"

"The KPD folks," my sister says. "Her group of friends. They had regular meetings to do communist things."

"Communist things like what?"

"Like learning Esperanto," my sister says. "Except Oma Lotte never learned, because her mother forbade her to go to the evening class. It wasn't political, Sophie was just against her daughter going out at night; she wanted to have her home."

My sister says Sophie's possessiveness spoiled Lotte's fun but saved her life: the Gestapo used the Esperanto class roster to find and deport her friends.

"Deport? Like, send abroad?"

"No," my sister says, "deportiert. Like, abgeholt."

I had known about the gay friend, had pictured my grandmother distraught to lose him, to lose her beautiful Jewish friend. I had never imagined most of her group of peers mown down. I never considered that, by the time she conceived my aunt, in January of 1937, her one right-leaning friend, my grandfather, might have been the only one left.

I HAVE CHECKED my sister's story: the Licht- und Luftbad as a place where women secretly talked politics. Exercise grew into a common pastime during the industrial revolution. Cycling, soccer, and gymnastics clubs became class-segregated nearly from the start, leaving workers to found their own. Because Nazi philosophy saw physical education as a way to demonstrate Aryan supremacy, even left-leaning sports clubs initially remained untouched by Gleichschaltung, the alignment of all public life under Nazi ideology. During the first few years after Hitler rose to power, some exercise establishments in working-class neighborhoods developed into hubs of communist or social democrat resistance. In between ball games, women plotted how to slip money and food to families of the "deported." JEWS NOT WELCOME HERE killed an island of resistance, a last refuge of political community.

HANS VON AACHEN'S renaissance nudes have names: Glanz, Blüte, Frohsinn—radiance, blossoming, joy. The choking part inside my soul, the part that makes me look away from joy because of bright-red danger signs, the part that won't permit the fullness of who I am, the part that dims my light—I owe her gratitude. I watch great-grandma Sophie pull a metal comb, relentless, through Lotte's snagging curls. I hear her throw a fit about her daughter's night-time Esperanto class, quenching her exuberance, saving her life.

To walk my own life's path means naming Sophie's voice. It means hearing the sound of Lotte's sandals plodding homeward across hot paving stones. It means the braided willow imprint on the skin below her elbow, the drag of currants uneaten in her basket, the weight of sugar, separate in its paper bag.

If I Died

Siyun Fang

If I disappear on your right side
one day in the future
please do not bury me
or place me in a box

If you pity me because of my fragility
please lay a thin layer of clean earth over me
so whenever I am awakened by insects in autumn,
I can hold trees by the arm and walk home
to see whether you still expose your toes
outside of the quilt

BLEACHED

Donna Hemans

PICTURE HIM: ALREADY old at twenty, face and neck bleached a sandy brown with store-bought bleaching cream, arms and ears still a deep brown, upper lip dark and now a stark contrast against his sandy brown face. His lips look like a smoker's. His jeans don't stretch across his lithe frame, but sit instead low on his hip, the crotch and thigh draping rather than pulled taut against his hip. His shirt is baggy, too large for his thin frame. Soon, he says, I'll be light-skinned and pretty. He doesn't laugh. His movements are exaggerated and defiant. His friend, quieter, already has brown eyes to match his bleached skin, evenly toned across the face and neck. It's Friday night karaoke at New Kingston's Hilton Hotel poolside and everyone comes out—uptown, downtown and people from the places in between. He claps at appropriate moments but what he's really doing is watching what the women wear, commenting with exaggerated sweeps of his head and hand on fabric and style and fit. A hesitant but beautiful voice croons a rendition of Roberta Flack's "Killing Me Softly with His Song." He dances, nodding his head as he moves, his gyrations purposeful and studied.

"You going to sing?" I ask.

"No," he says. "Karaoke is for the brave." He looks me dead in the eyes as if I were a potential mate. "You brave?"

"Brave, yes," I say, "but I don't sing in public."

Tonight, I have no noble intentions. That's where my bravado lies. I am with a girl who, at twenty-one, is nearer his age than mine. Tanya is a dark-skinned beauty with a runner's body, a young woman flattered by a middle-aged man's attention. She is uncomfortable with this young man's bleached skin. I, on the other hand, am already thinking of him as one of our country's lost boys. I specialize in youths like him and families struggling to stay together. He is what I have been looking for: a challenge. Tanya whispers something about the beauty of the pink and white and purple drooping bell flowers in the garden surrounding the pool. Her muscled arms and soft breasts lean into me.

"Yes, beautiful," I say.

She looks at me hard and I know that she thinks I am thinking of her breasts and arms brushing my body. I am. She says she needs a drink. I unfold the bills and let her go. Had I been more attentive, I would have directed her to one of the empty garden chairs ringing the pool and surprised her with a fruity drink blended with crushed ice and rum.

Tanya walks away. From behind she looks like she could be a young boy or a pre-teen girl. It tickles me to imagine what the boy beside me thinks.

He calls himself Lesley. He lives with his father in a zinced tenement yard in Whitfield Town. His three chances out of Whitfield Town and into an uptown life, he thinks, lie in music and dance and his newly lightened skin. I know otherwise. He watches the singer on stage, his mouth slightly open, then says the woman could have a career in music if only she wanted it. His mother lives in Stewart Town at the base of an old high school for girls, where she works laundering and cooking for the girls who board there. He wants to be in neither of the places his parents live, Stewart Town nor Kingston, preferring instead north coast towns—Ocho Rios, Runaway Bay or Montego Bay.

"More possibilities," he says, without explaining.

He sings snatches of songs, punctuating his words with hand movements and a simple sway of his body. He talks and I watch. He names the dancers he knows and the music videos they have appeared in. But he says nothing about where or how these new dancers live or how long he thinks their dance careers will last.

Tanya's body brushes mine. She gestures to two empty seats.

"Give me a call if you ever want to talk," I say to Lesley, extending my hand with two business cards between my thumb and forefinger.

I shadow Tanya's thin and lithe body that I imagine will one day develop a woman's curves. She doesn't lean into me as I wish she would but holds her body as if she wants nothing to do with me. Six songs later, Lesley is on the stage. His voice isn't nearly as beautiful as some of the others. Without the music and vocals in the background the sound wouldn't be beautiful at all. But he performs as if he belongs there, his body fluid and movement rhythmic. There is bravery, I think.

THE MUSIC FALLS away. The silence is incomplete. Tanya leans in and kisses my cheek, not giving me a chance at all to circle my arms around her waist or kiss her lips. It is a familiar routine now. The young beauty I dated two weeks earlier told me simply that in my presence she felt like a helpless child and not a grown woman.

"How so?" I asked.

"This," she said, her arms spread wide. "You're telling me to walk on the inside, away from the traffic. And yes, it's the proper thing for a gentleman to do. But I feel like a child. My father used to do that."

And then I understood. She wasn't truly uncomfortable with what I did but with my age, my forty-two year-old self.

The night passes quickly, thanks to a complimentary bottle of yam wine, the fan that whirs overhead, the mosquitoes that buzz and flit, breaking the silence of the night.

FIVE DAYS LATER, Lesley comes to my office wearing the same tight pants and baggy shirt. There's a bruise near his left eye and he walks with a distinct limp. Here is something he hasn't practiced. The limp is the most natural thing about him.

"What happened to you?"

"Nothing."

I want to believe the bruises are from an innocent fight but I think only of something more disturbing. "Okay," I say. "We don't have to talk about it."

"You gave me your card." He holds the card in his hand, worrying the edges with his fingers. He stands, walks to the window, the swaying of his body exaggerated.

"So you understand," I say, "I prefer women."

He doesn't turn away from the window, but his shoulders drop and he straightens his legs a little. When he turns around, he remains by the window, his back to the light, his eyes asking the question his mouth won't.

"I think of business cards as insurance. Maybe I don't need a lawyer today. But who knows what I'll need next week or next year. Maybe I don't need a musician tomorrow, but maybe in a year I'll need a pianist to play at my wedding. Just the same, you never know when you might need my help."

He stares at the plaques on the wall, the certificates of appreciation from the Kiwanis Club of New Kingston, the Rotary Club of Jamaica, the St. Andrew High School for Girls, his eyes lingering on each and his lips mouthing the words as he reads what's written on each.

"So what exactly you do here?" he asks.

"I help families. That's the simplest way to put it."

"How?"

"That depends on who needs help. I counsel children or parents individually or the children and parents together. A family is like a band. The drum has to be in harmony with the keyboard or the horn or the guitar. The children have to be in harmony with the mother and the father. One person might sometimes play off key but the band needs to be able to play together. That's what I do. I help the band play together."

His thin fingers wipe away oil and a film of sweat from his forehead and the creases by the side of his nose. He doesn't know how long it took me to come up with that analogy of a family being like a band. But I use it because it works with the young and sometimes with the old.

"A man nearly kill me," he says, dropping his body into the chair before the desk. He speaks as if each word carries a distinct weight.

"What happened?"

He laces his thin fingers together. His fingers are dark, the true shade of his natural skin. He hasn't begun bleaching the remainder of his body. Not yet.

"Can't stay here," he says instead. "I have to leave Kingston."

"Where do you want to go?"

"I don't know. Anywhere."

"You must want something specific," I say.

"I'll go anywhere."

He fiddles with the toys on my desk—the stress relief rubber ball, the foam basketball and hoop set, the plastic hammer, the canned Play Doh. Gone is the bravado of Friday night, a bravado that was either battered out of him or a bravado that was present only in the presence of the stage and the forgiving audience.

"Here," I say. "Write your name and the date and below that, write your biggest dream. Something you want to do, a place you want to visit, a person you want to meet."

He writes continuously for five minutes, turning the index card over and writing as well on the back. He doesn't make a list but writes one long paragraph. The words, though, are too small for me to read from my side of the desk. I don't interrupt the conscious flow.

"Finished," he says as if he's solved a great puzzle or is certain he's got the answer right.

"That's yours," I say. "Hold on to it. Look these over and tomorrow we'll talk about some possibilities for you."

He scans the papers—sheets describing vocational training schools and programs that ready yet more of our youths for hotel and hospitality work. I in turn scan my watch, for I am to meet another young beauty in time for drinks at a roof-top bar in Constant Spring.

"Ten o'clock?" I ask.

"Yes, sir."

He's almost out the door, hobbling, and I wish I had asked what he wrote. Instead, I ask, "How much money do you need?" He doesn't answer directly. I walk as if to close the door and hand him a crisp $1,000 bill.

"Ten o'clock," I say.

The beauty, Sharon, I am to meet, doesn't turn up at all. She calls as I am starting my second beer to say she has to babysit her sick sister's daughters. It's not the worst excuse I've heard but I can't help but think that I, who counsel families on building relationships, and youth on finding their place in the world, am failing at creating for myself the very thing I promote.

I sip the beer and watch the uptown scene. There are no bleached faces here. In fact, there doesn't seem to be a merging of Kingston's uptown and downtown crowd. The women are nearly flawless and perfectly styled, all looking like transplants from a hip New York or Miami scene. I like the consciously artsy ones, the group of three with natural, untamed, spiral curls, jewelry that tinkles and jangles, skirts that flow and reveal all at the same time. They're young and fresh, not yet hardened by life's disappointments. I think of Lesley, his newly lightened skin and affected attitude, which he believes will be an invitation to this aspect of Kingston's uptown life. But he wouldn't fit in here.

AT EIGHT-THIRTY, Lesley is already present. The natural early-morning light isn't kind to his skin. The contrast between the lightened and darker skin is too great. There are two red spots on his right cheek that could be bruises or the skin blotched and already damaged by the bleaching creams.

"You should see a doctor about those red spots," I say.

He puts his hand to his cheek and looks at me cautiously as if he expects me to say more about his efforts to lighten his skin. But I won't. It's not my place. He remains outside perched on the low stone wall between an ornamental grass and a frangipani tree that refuses to grow. Inside, I open up the windows, wipe away the film of black dust that filters in daily through the open windows, and refresh the plants with yesterday's stale coffee. Coffee might even be toxic to the plants but I am my mother's son. She didn't like waste.

Lesley gives me ten minutes and then he comes in with a stalk of the ornamental grass. He pauses near a still-plump anthurium flower and drops the stalk into the water beside it. Inside my office, he moves the chair closer to the window and drops his body as if he has no energy left to carry it.

"Tell me," I begin, "of the dream you wrote yesterday."

Lesley fidgets with his bag, opens a folder that seems to have once contained a school project and hands me a sheet of paper. On the sheet is a penciled image of me, my arm around a young thing that could be either male or female. He filled in few details of the male figure's companion, but he perfected the details of my face, capturing my full cheeks and broad nose, my ears that curve outward, the single chain I wear around my neck.

"Damn," I say. "When did you do this?"

"Weekend." He pulls another sheet from the battered folder. "Last night," he says as he hands the second sheet to me.

Again, the details are sharp and the face is unmistakably mine. But in the second, I don't think of the male figure simply as a man, but as a father reaching across the desk to someone not captured by the artist at all. There is concern on the face. I wish the women I've known could see this deep concern, passion, yearning in me too. Here is this boy who seems indirectly to be asking me to treat him as a son.

"You're good, naturally good."

"Thank you."

"You should be in art school," I say and let the words hang. "Now, why do you want to leave Kingston?"

"Kingston is too small for me."

I wish he would say more, but he is adept at deflecting my questions and saying only that which he wants to say. This is quite a skill for one so young. "Where do you want to go?"

"The north coast."

"Why the north coast?"

"Life is bigger there."

He has it backwards, I think. But he may be looking at life with an artist's eye and seeing something that I wouldn't otherwise see.

"Art school is here," I say. "You'll have plenty of time to live your life elsewhere."

That, of course, isn't what he wants to hear. He drops his gaze to the floor, then looks up and reaches out a hand for the drawings.

"I can draw," he says. "No teacher can teach me that."

His hand is still outstretched.

"Can I hold onto these?"

He pulls his hand back, but says nothing.

I had underestimated him. Perhaps I hoped he would fold under my wisdom.

Maybe that's my problem with women. Perhaps I look for the younger women because I want them not only to need me, but to fold under my wisdom as well.

"I'll make a deal with you," I say quickly, not wanting to lose him. "I'll get you into a training program on the north coast, whatever program you like, if you agree to meet sometimes with an artist. Nothing formal. Just meet, talk, and let him look at your work."

It doesn't take him long to choose bartending.

"Sooner or later everybody drinks," he says.

Lesley's footsteps are still echoing down the hall when I pick up the phone to call the artist, Fred.

I SKIP THE outdoor bars in favor of a Thursday night poetry reading. Tanya is the first person I see. She walks toward me slowly, eyes widening with surprise.

"Didn't expect to see you here," she says.

"Does that mean you wouldn't have come if you had expected to see me?"

"I didn't say that."

"I know."

"Everything all right?"

"Everything's good. No worries."

She allows my arm to rest on her waist but once we sit she pulls her chair away from the table and away from me, forcing me to lean forward to talk. Her eyes scan the growing crowd. So far there isn't a hint of age or gray in the crowd.

"There's Paul," she says.

Paul looks around the room and comes right over.

"Nervous?" Tanya asks before he even settles.

"Not really." He extends a clammy, sweaty hand to me and says his name. "Dexter," I say. "So you're a poet?"

"I don't call myself a poet," he says. "At least, I won't until I have a book." Four more join us. Their drinks crowd the small table. Except for me, no one at the table works. Four are pursuing a second degree. The poet is planning to attend graduate school abroad and Tanya hasn't decided if she wants to manage her father's business or pursue studies abroad. The second oldest among us is twenty-two. They're vibrant and fresh, wearing their youthfulness like splash-on cologne.

The poets are loud, some mediocre, some good. Paul is among the good ones, but his work is predictable and could still be better. I excuse myself before the poetry ends.

At home, my footsteps echo loudly on the new ceramic tiles. I wish for carpeting or wood floors to soften the sounds of my loneliness. I look over Lesley's pictures, imagining a wooden frame and dark matting. All my recent relationships are captured in this single moment drawn by an amateur artist. I picture again what he sees: a middle-aged man with his arm around a woman so young, so fresh she could still be wearing socks and shoes and a pleated high school uniform. If this is what he sees, then what do the women see? Do they see a father or a husband or a friend?

Sleep doesn't come as I wish. I lie in bed worrying I won't ever marry or have children of my own. The families and children I counsel are all I'll ever have. I acknowledge though that I want Lesley to also be like Tanya's crowd, to wear his youthfulness and energy without care, to shelve the wariness that he carries in front of him like a burdensome armor. Mostly, though, I want him to be as proud as last night's poets, to flaunt his talent without reservation. I am thinking like a father, imagining a gallery opening and reception, his work hanging in the National Gallery of Art in a revitalized downtown and Lesley showing off the skills that got him there.

LESLEY'S ADDRESS ISN'T easy to find. The street sign is bending to the grass and the house numbers aren't bold or prominent. A child dressed in uniform and on her way to school points in the direction of four houses, all sloping, three with blue tarpaulin shading the verandahs from the sun or covering hurricane-damaged walls and windows. Lesley's father isn't what I imagined him to be. He's past sixty but carrying with him the defined and bulky muscles of a thirty- or forty-year-old. He is bending over the cab of a truck, black grease coating his elbows and hands.

Lesley's father makes no attempt to shake my hand and looks up only once to glance at the drawings I want him to see.

"Man mus' have money to live," he says, pointing to a truck. "See the truck there waiting for him to get his license. Two, three years time me and him will build a big trucking business. Five, six trucks. Five, six drivers. Then he can sit back and draw all he want."

There's a swarm of tiny flies. He swats at them, bending over once again to attend to the greasy engine.

"Down here, we don' have time for that kin' o' luxury."

Down here. Once he separates my perceived uptown life from his I know I am dismissed. His dismissal is nothing that I can't bear and surprisingly not a dismissal at all.

PICTURE US: A light-skinned forty-two-year-old man, bald and sofening around the middle; and a seventeen-year-old with bleached skin, close-cropped hair with curls loosened by a chemical texturizer, a pair of large cubic zirconium knobs in his pierced ears, and wearing close-fitting blue jeans and a baggy shirt that make him look soft and effeminate. The older man, in relaxed blue jeans and a white polo shirt, steers the youth away from the fashions popular with the dancehall music video dancers, away from the pants that fit like fruit peel. The older man stands outside the fitting room door, approving what he sees with a slight nod. Once, he steps away to fetch a larger size. The older man pays with a credit card. The youth, not yet transformed, holds the plastic shopping bags to his chest. Father and son? Lovers?

We don't talk about his father or my unannounced visit and I try not to think at all why I have got so involved in this boy's life. My mind says I shouldn't be so involved. But my heart says I should. I tell myself this is my way of repaying a debt owed to a teacher who saved me from myself, not by taking me in, but by forcing me to see how effort and hard work can make a mediocre student seem like a natural scholar. Even now I sometimes rub the rough skin that formed on my finger one afternoon from writing and rewriting an essay until I got it right. She didn't change my grade, but read the essay aloud to the class and mounted it in a corner of the room. I owe her a debt and I'll repay it.

Lesley changes in my office and we leave just before midday for Runaway Bay for an interview at the Heart Academy where he'll learn his trade. I take the back road through Red Hills to bypass Spanish Town, where rival gangs are warring again after a child was shot accidentally at her gate. Nothing short of more bullets will appease the gangsters. The police think so too for they are eliminating the dons, whose gangs control parcels of each community, one by one by one. I don't watch the news anymore. Night after night there's a parent bawling. And day after day there's a parent in my office hoping to block off a wayward child's destructive path before it is too late.

Lesley takes one look at the youths in training and decides immediately that hospitality work isn't what he wants to do. There is no glory in the job.

"Serve, serve, serve," he says.

I can't picture him in the elevated cab of a tractor trailer or dump truck. Even now, dressed in relaxed blue jeans and a blue buttoned shirt, he still looks soft and a little unprepared for the world. We sit outside the Heart Hotel, Lesley looking off at two uniformed girls walking away from the hotel, and a group of guests getting onto a tour bus.

"Do you want..."

"Nothing to do with this," he says, anticipating my question before I even finish.

"What's your next move?" I ask.

"Don't know yet," he says. "You are the counselor."

"Monday we have a meeting with the artist I mentioned," I say.

He neither accepts nor rejects my proposition but straightens his body and starts walking toward the car. The ride back is mostly silent. The engine hums, the sound muted by the closed windows and air conditioner. We are nearing Red Hills again when I ask if he has ever studied the works of other artists.

"Studied?"

"Yes. I mean, have you ever gone to the gallery and looked at what other artists do?"

"No."

"It's right downtown."

"You don't have to tell me. I know where."

Still I want to help this boy.

I leave the car in front of the office without going in. There should be a client inside and an indifferent secretary, occasionally telling the client that I will be there shortly, and chewing on fruit and crackers. We take a taxi. The driver, an older man missing most of his teeth, is listening to a woman on the radio talking about hardship and the trials of her life. He turns to me. "What's your testimony?" he asks.

"Testimony?" I can think only of the elders in a church revival meeting telling of how they came to know the Lord. "I don't have one."

"Everybody has a testimony. Me, I believe three things make for a good life. First one is hard work. Think of a job. Anything you think of I can do it. Second is good food. Seventy years now I living and I have no heart problems, no pressure, no sugar. None o' them things. And you know what the third one is." He glances at me and in the rear view mirror at Lesley. Lesley isn't paying attention. "The third is plenty sex."

I should have expected that, but I smile.

"Yes, sex. Nine children I have," he says. "You have children?"

"No," I say.

Immediately, he looks up and back again at Lesley's bleached face in the rearview mirror, as if he has decided what we are. He is silent the rest of the way. And I want to say "Son," to change for a minute this man's perception of me. When we get out of the taxi,

Lesley takes my hand, and bends forward as if to speak to the driver. He lets go of my hand only after the tires squeal. Once again with somebody watching he regains his bravado, puts on his public face.

Lesley doesn't look at the paintings as hungrily as I hoped he would. He shuffles along slowly, looking at each but paying no particular attention to any one style. He lingers at an installation of a ghetto street, complete with graffitied zinc sheets lining a narrow passage, political slogans, tires, trash, and a layer of dust. The realistic ghetto street is set up like a winding maze. In the middle is a stuffed body, the legs bent haphazardly at the knee.

"This is a no art," he says. "Unless you saying art is what is real."

"That's why you need to study art," I say.

He lingers over the sculptures, his hand reaching forward as if he wants to caress the wood and stone. He turns back the way we came, purposeful. He knows what he wants to return to see. I linger for a while in the area of the sculptures, before returning to the ghetto scene. Lesley, when I catch up to him, is looking intently at a penciled drawing of an elongated body that to my untrained eye is a whimsical yet detailed piece of work. I know now that I have convinced him that art school is a possibility.

There are purposeful footsteps coming through the gallery. It's closing time. Outside, the after-work crowd downtown has already thinned. Lesley points to the waterfront and I point to a restaurant. From the restaurant I watch a group of aimless boys, barefoot, ragged. They hassle a man and I hear the echo of curses, the older man's threats.

We don't linger over dinner—pumpkin rice and jerk chicken. Soon, we are walking in the shadow of old wooden buildings, heading toward the waterfront. The boys are back. A group of seven, some older, some younger, all ragged and barefoot.

"Beg you a money," one says.

I search my pockets for a $20 coin. Paper bills scratch my palm.

"Sorry," I say. "Don't have anything this time."

From the boys, I hear the words I had never used to describe Lesley and words I didn't think anyone would ever use to describe me. Lesley says something, his retort sounding like a comeback he'd once wished he had said and then practiced fervently after. It doesn't matter to me whether they think of him as my son or lover. I want my life and body intact. The biggest of the boys grabs for Lesley's bag. I throw myself at him and just as I feel my fist connecting with bone, I wonder what I'm doing, how I've come to this—a street fight with ragged, dirty boys. But it's too late. Voices rise up from around us, sounding then like echoes in a hollow room. The biggest of the boys lunges at me. He doesn't touch me but I feel my foot slipping, my body going down and the solid, hard concrete beneath me. Then nothing.

A NURSE PUSHES a wheel-chaired patient. Another administers an injection. Things slowly become unblurred. Lesley is hovering over the bed, looking at me as if my movement is the strangest thing. A bandage covers his right eye. The other is swollen, the lids bulging like a clove of garlic. His left fingers are bandaged, taped together like a hand in a mitten. My memory of the events doesn't return slowly, but so rapidly my head throbs where it hit the concrete.

"You don't look so good," I say. "You should see yourself."

I try to say something else but he begs me to hush. He says it so quietly I can barely hear. He has no audience, no reason to show off. He sits down, slouching backward. He nods at me and I nod in return. He points to a bouquet but says nothing and doesn't move to hand me the card. He says he is going to live with his mother for now.

"What about art school?"

"Art school isn't for me. Besides, country better for me right now."

"Your father?" I ask.

He says nothing but lets his one good eye wander as if he must control everything within sight. He gets up from the chair, hobbles away from my direct gaze.

Tanya is the only person I call. When she answers her cell phone, her voice is breathy as if she's been running or walking fast. "I'll come right over," she says when I tell her I'm in the hospital. It doesn't bother me that her concern might be pity. It bothers me that there is no one else to call, no child of my own, no wife. What I want most is a woman's touch, her breath against my skin, her mouth so close I can imagine a soft kiss. A nurse comes and goes.

Lesley looks out the window as if he is waiting for something to happen. He barely moves. He shifts his weight from one leg to another, but he doesn't turn around or acknowledge me.

Tanya, when she comes, looks at Lesley's back, then at me, and shakes her head. "I knew this was going to be trouble," she says. She doesn't look again at Lesley. She moves quickly, seemingly without effort. She hands me a bottle of coconut water, then holds it while I sip through a straw. Her scent is a combination of powder and rose. I close my eyes, imagining just the two of us, her fingers still brushing my chin.

"Picture me ten years from now," Lesley says suddenly, his voice falling from a place above my head. "Honestly, what do you see?"

My head is throbbing, but I try to take control of the conversation. It isn't my place to tell him how his life will turn out but to guide him where he wants to go. But Tanya is here and I want her to see me at my fullest, to see me as a more-than-capable man. "Picture yourself," I say. "What do you see?"

"Nothing," he says. "I can't see myself at all."

As he talks, he slowly circles the bed. He is not performing now. I see his skin, bleached, the subtle gradations of change in color. A bleached boy, no longer dark brown but perhaps in a few years his skin will be the color of sand. It's not his skin that he really wants to change. It's something else inside. His life is in my hands. I see him for what he is: a naked and vulnerable young man, pliable still. I see our small island for what it is: a place that can harm such a man.

"Picture this," I say. I close my eyes to shut out Tanya's face, the way she looks at Lesley as if he's nothing more than scum. I can imagine her, instead, looking at me with something other than pity, her face softened with a feeling bordering on love. My voice is slow and deliberate. I hold up my hands to shape a box. "Ten years from now, the caption under a photograph will read, 'Jamaican artist Lesley Forbes presents a painting to the prime minister.' Still another will read, 'Jamaican artist Lesley Forbes donates work to the National Museum of Art.'"

He is quiet as I speak, his breath even. I don't think of myself as a hero or savior. I don't think of myself as a potential lover of the girl I want to impress. I want to think of myself solely as a mature man who has lived years these two haven't yet seen. It is I who am on the stage now, performing. What I say doesn't make me proud, but I speak anyway, my eyes closed, the words filling the space between us, the boy he is bleached completely and the shape of a man emerging.

PICTURE ME AS a young man his age. Maybe you can't.

Picture Lesley now. Still yet, maybe you can't.

A LANGUAGE OF MY OWN

Jesus Francisco Sierra

LESS THAN TWO weeks after I left Havana in 1969, I began 7th grade at Horace Mann Middle School in San Francisco. I was placed in a bilingual class held in a large trailer by the far corner of the schoolyard. Our teacher, Miss Cuevas, a slender soft-spoken woman from El Salvador, paced the front of the room. She spoke Spanish with a deliberate, paused cadence. A chubby kid, so short his feet didn't reach the ground, sat in the front row and raised his hand.

"Miss Cuevas," he said, "how will I know when I've learned English?"

She paused and considered the question. "When you dream in English," she said.

In San Francisco the weather, like the people and their way, was cold. The language sounded unintelligible. Even the Spanish was different. The same words were used but they carried a different rhythm, a different bounce. Still, growing up in the Mission District I dreamt mostly in Spanish—it was difficult not to. It was all I spoke at home and with friends. Saturday mornings across the street from my house, my friend Raymond would perch his large speakers on the window ledge of his second floor flat. He'd angle them toward the street and crank out salsa music loud enough to wake up the entire neighborhood. I listened and mouthed the Spanish lyrics while I danced alone in my room.

Perhaps dancing was my way of trying to reclaim that joy so radically muted when I left the island.

I've spent most of my life since then in San Francisco. The neighborhood sound that most defined my generation, and my American self, was the music of bands like Santana, Malo, War, and Tower of Power. Their mix of soul, jazz, funk, and rock, driven by the pulsating rhythms of Latin music, told the story of us. I danced to that music too. The neighborhood was itself a fusion of people from different worlds, heavily rooted in the Latino culture that most defined it. The music echoed the edgy and often rough character of the Mission, a working-class community trying to survive and thrive in their new home. It reflected the revolutionary inheritance of a community where many of the residents had been displaced from their home countries by revolutions of their own. The dance steps revealed not only defiance and anger, but also resilience.

I was eighteen years old when, on a Friday night in September of 1977, I went to a garage party with my friends Ramon, a handsome, tall, blue-eyed Mexican, and Tommy, a sullen-looking, weight-lifting teen born to a Swiss father and a Salvadoran mother. The garage—on the ground level of a two-story, early 1950s stucco house near Alemany Boulevard—was dimly lit by a single purple light bulb at the back of the room. It reeked of cheap stale beer and cigarette smoke. Tommy and I had killed a half pint of Pinch Scotch we'd bought earlier at Rossi's Liquors on 24th Street, a place that had been busted several times for selling liquor to minors but always managed to reopen weeks later. Ramon didn't drink; he never did. A small turntable sat on top of the washer near the door that led to the backyard, playing Santana's *Evil Ways*. Two boys with long hair and a girl wearing tight bell-bottomed jeans flipped through a stack of 45s and argued about what to play next.

I eyed a girl sitting on a metal folding chair against the garage door. I walked over with my best 'nobody fucks with me' stroll, chest out, shoulders back, swinging my right arm only slightly, my head tilted back, chin up. I asked her to dance. She stood with certain resolve and not a hint of hesitation. She wore tight, fusia-colored jeans and a black vest over a beige short-sleeved blouse. I saw her high cheekbones, dark hair, and almond eyes. Like most of the kids at the party, she was Latina. She was pretty. Her name was Connie.

I had to look cool and tough. My dance moves slow and deliberate, emulating the control and authority I needed to display. I danced with restrained movements as if making sure to state my boundaries, perhaps a physical display not just of my budding machohood and requisite badassness, but of my reluctance to accept that different version of me, of my life in this new country.

Connie's swing proved different: sexier, reserved, but loose enough for her to smile as we moved to the music about a foot apart from each other. We both seemed firm in something that, after our arduous journeys North, we were unwilling to concede: space. It was our space. It was our dance. It wasn't new, but it was singularly our own. But I struggled. I questioned whether this fresh dance form betrayed who I was and where I came from. I was Cuban, damn it! This was not how I danced!

I felt this new music in a different part of my body. When I first heard the conga drum riff at the start of Santana's *Soul Sacrifice*, my jaw tightened and my legs stiffened. The sound stung me in a familiar place, tapping the inside of my ribcage like a mallet.

I snapped my fingers to the beat when I danced, a habit I'd picked up from my father before he died. It's one of the few things I remember about him: how he snapped his fingers to the jazz he heard on the radio in early 1960's Havana, illegally tuned to a Miami radio station.

"That's real music," he'd tell me.

Now, I allowed the tropical sound embedded in Santana's music to move me. I pressed my thumb and middle fingers to a beat-matching snap.

Tower of Power's *So Very Hard To Go* played next. I reached for Connie's hand and brought her close to me. She embraced me and rested her head on my shoulder. Her closeness seemed to break through that veil of toughness I had to maintain, lest the other dudes in the place sense weakness. My legs weakened a bit, and my heart raced as I inhaled the freshness of her hair and sensed the warmth of her breath against the shield that was my chest. I wrapped my arms around her. My shoulders seemed to ease under the weight of her feathery touch. We rocked slow in unison to the lyrics:

Ain't nothin' I can say, nothin' I can do,
I feel so bad, yeah, I feel so blue.
I got to make it right for everyone concerned
even if it's me, if it means it's me...

In time, the more I heard it coming out of cars, at parties, and on the radio, the more it birthed new memories with these new friends. This new language began to inhabit my dreams and silence the memory of my childhood in that other place.

In May of 1997, my mother and I returned to Havana, where I'd spent the first twelve years of my life. I'd been away from Cuba for twenty-eight years. By then I'd been dreaming in English for twenty-six. Cuba, a place steeped in mystery, was still clawing its way out of the Periodo Especial—the period after the Berlin Wall fell and the Russians stopped subsidizing the island's economy. The stench of rotten food and diesel exhaust was everywhere. I wondered if I'd just forgotten the smell of my youth, or if the overwhelming sight of my family, or the land I thought I'd never see again, had heightened my senses.

On the drive from the airport I hung my arm outside the car window. My eyes fixed on the passing Havana landscape, houses, and people, as if seeing it all for the first time. I saw neglected mounds of garbage dotting the roadside. We drove through potholed streets to the corner of 15th and A streets in Lawton, the Havana neighborhood where my mother's side of the family had lived for over ninety years. My eighty-year-old aunt, Tia Kiki, squeezed next to me in the back seat of my cousin's Moskovich (the signature Russian car of the times). She held my hand.

"Not enough gas for the garbage trucks to run regularly," she said, looking up to me with a loving, toothless smile. "But we make do."

As we drove along, despite the hunger and despair, I heard music blaring from homes, cars, bars, restaurants, and on the street.

"I'm glad you're here," Tia Kiki said when we arrived at her house.

Hearing the beat in her voice and the rapid-fire language of everyone around me, I wondered if this was still my Spanish. It must have been, because the instant I'd stepped across the threshold of the airplane door, I'd discarded English as if it had outlived its usefulness. It happened with the immediacy of someone fleeing a storm, rushing into a home and slamming the door behind him, lest the winds and rain come in and destroy it all.

My mother and I spent the day surrounded by family. An incessant parade of first, second and third cousins, their kids, old neighbors. Many of my mother's old friends stopped by to talk to us, or to see if there was a chance we might part with a gift for them.

By two in the morning, after twenty-eight years of lost time thrust upon us in a single day, I sat on the front porch of my Tia Kiki's house exhausted, trying to reconcile my absence. I sipped the last of Havana Club Rum someone had brought. My mother rocked in the same metal rocking chair her mother had rocked in many years before. She crossed one arm across her chest, as if holding in the ache of memory. She held her other hand up to her mouth with her index finger resting lightly on her thin upper lip, perhaps encouraging her own silence. I'd seen this many times before. It was what she did when she was deep in thought.

Except for the music echoing off the tall living room walls inside the house, the dark Lawton neighborhood corner of 15th and A street was quiet and deserted. I watched my cousin's twenty-four year-old daughter, Maguy, dance in front of us with her husband Carlos. She shrugged her slender shoulders and said, "What else are we going to do?"

Carlos' pale skin glistened with a thin layer of sweat. Against Maguy's golden skin and short black hair, his skin seemed lighter than it was. The unusual way their steps syncopated with the music made their movements seem smoother. The turns flowed with an ease that helped me better understand the music, the people, and myself.

"It's either this, or we cry ourselves to sleep," she added.

Their mirrored movements were far from choreographed. They glided across the floor with obvious confidence. Their sure smiles seemed to articulate an understanding that having shared such difficult times together, this triumphant physical expression was a creation all their own. It was their story of perseverance, taking them to a place where they could exist without hunger, reprisal, or hopelessness.

Watching and listening revived a part of me that I'd long ago given up for lost. It might have been the simple remembrance of my youth, but I decided it was the recognition of a shared past being dissolved in that music and dance.

A skinny young man with closely cropped hair, wearing jean shorts and a tattered sport coat—too hot to wear in the stifling Havana heat—walked by and stopped in front of the house. Sweat streaked down the side of his face.

He leaned in over the railing that bordered the front porch and said, "Buenas noches. You dance well."

"Buenas noches," we said.

My cousin and her husband continued to dance.

The young man turned his head to either side then said, "I've got steaks."

Maguy and Carlos stopped dancing. The man pulled one side of his sport coat open to reveal two large steaks wrapped in bloody newspaper. My mother shook her head. Her eyes welled with tears. As if pulled down by the weight of them, she dropped her head and wept. I drank the last of my rum and swallowed hard.

A couple of days later I visited my uncle, Tio Rene. He lived alone in a small ground-floor apartment, on Patrocinio Street in La Vibora, a different Havana neighborhood—where my father grew up. Tio Rene was the only one of the four brothers on my father's side who remained. In his seventies by then, he was still a musician and superb dancer. Restless, just as I remembered him, Tio Rene gave me a hurried hug while he fought back tears. He said I reminded him of his brother, my father, who died in 1965 before we left Cuba all those years before.

"Sientate. We have a lot to talk about," he said, pointing to the worn couch in the front room.

A guitar, its strings straight and orderly, with its delicate laminated wooden face, leaned on the wall next to the couch and shone with the brilliance of a virgin mirror. He made his way to the kitchen, weaving around shoes strewn on the living room floor, pushing aside out-of-place chairs draped with wrinkled shirts. I picked up an old newspaper from the seat cushion and sat on the couch. I watched him walk away and remembered how years ago my six-year-old brother and I had struggled to keep up with his long strides as he dragged us through the meandering walks of Parque Almendares. His strides seemed shorter now, and slower.

"I'll make us some coffee so we can talk," he said.

We sipped coffee. He asked about me, my sister—whose mention always brought tears to his eyes—and my brother. How do you explain to someone what twenty-eight years of exile from home, from family, from friends, and from an irreversible history feels like? I didn't try. Instead, I told him about my life, what I'd lost, and how abandoned I'd felt at first. I found it difficult to explain my American life in Spanish. Just as I'd discarded my English upon arriving, I felt as though I'd cast off my American life, perhaps angry upon realizing that I'd been led astray from what my life should have been. And now I was back. Being American felt as distant and obscure as it did before I left.

He told me about his difficult life and his failing health. "But that's life," he said.

He waved his hand across his face as if swatting something away. "I'm all fucked up. But I'm happy." He reached for the guitar. "You want to hear a song?"

He crossed one leg over the other and rested the guitar's belly on his thigh. Leaning his head to the side he regarded the guitar's long neck as one would a lover. A soft, settling sound filled the room when he ran his fingers across the taut, finely tuned strings. He paused and inhaled a long profound breath as if attempting to exhume a lost time. He closed his eyes and looked up. In his deep, velvety voice, he sang boleros he'd written over the years. The music made the steamy apartment feel breezy, lightening the burden of absence that had, until then, lingered between us.

Certain music binds itself to the memory of such homecomings. As much as my uncle's songs, for me, it was the sound of Son 14. As I was readying to leave, my Tio Rene asked me to wait. I watched him amble back down the narrow hall to his bedroom. He emerged minutes later holding a portable cassette player. He sat and pressed a button. The music played. The sound was unlike the assertive, brassy New York sounds of iconic bands that brought salsa music to the mainstream in the seventies and eighties, like Willie Colon and the Fania All-Stars. This was different. Incorporating the drum set and the synthesizer, not typical for that music, it had a funkier swing.

"I want you to have it," he said.

He popped the tape out of the player and handed it to me. He wrapped his callused hands around mine and pressed tight. He aimed his prominent nose at me and without the hint of a smile said, "Listen to it, enjoy it, and don't ever lose it. Don't forget, we're Cuban!"

My Tio Rene was bound to the music, and the music was bound to him. Cuba was bound to both—and to me.

In the final days of that trip, I spent an afternoon with a few childhood friends. We sat poolside and sipped beers at Rio Crystal, where I'd learned to swim as a kid. It sits at the base of a berm below Boyeros, a highway that connects central Havana to the Jose Marti Airport and beyond. While we sat, talked, and shared memories, trying to reconstruct our past, a car stopped on the road above. The car doors opened. We heard music playing. Two couples stepped out of the car and danced on the side of the road until the song stopped. They laughed, got back in the car, and drove off.

One of my friends turned to me and said, "I bet you don't see *that* over there."

"No, we don't," I said.

No, I don't, I thought.

BACK IN SAN Francisco, a few years after that trip, a friend called to ask if I'd come with him to see a touring Cuban band, Jesus Alemany's *Cubanismo*. They were playing two shows in Emeryville, just over the bridge from San Francisco. Entangled in an emotionally debilitating divorce, I didn't have the energy. I hadn't gone out alone in a while, but eventually my reluctance yielded to my friend's insistence, and I decided to go.

I arrived early to a venue vibrating with the rolling murmur of an expectant crowd. A large elevated stage overlooked a small dance floor enclosed by a semicircle of tables and booths. I decided to stand against the wall along the side aisle that led down to the dance floor. I scanned the audience looking for my friend but didn't see him.

The MC announced the band to a cheering audience as the musicians filed onto the stage. With a four-man horn section, percussion, bass, drum set, piano, and three vocalists, this wasn't a band—it was a full orchestra. When the first note blasted out, it felt like the sound elevated me, searing a hole in the sky for me to travel through time. Part of me took flight. I leapt off the wall. I hurried down to the edge of the stage. I asked a woman to dance. She was a slender blond with narrow cheeks that lifted as her thin lips parted into a smile. I slipped my right hand around her waist and lifted her other hand shoulder high. I gently guided her into the first step, to the beat. She followed my lead with ease, her movements subtle but certain. She smiled. Cuban or not, she shared the groove enough so that I imagined myself dancing at my aunt's front porch in Lawton. I pictured my Tio Rene's vivid eyes and wide smile as he strummed his guitar, sang, and swayed to his own music. He nodded at me knowingly, happy that his gifts to me survived, that they saved him, and saved me.

THE LAST FRIDAY of every month for more than fifteen years, Il Pirata, a small bar on 16th Street in San Francisco, hosts a Cuban dance party. Over the front door, a vertical blade sign spells Il Pirata in glowing green neon letters.

On the way in, I stop at the bar and order eighteen-year Flor de Caña rum, neat. I sip it and make my way into the other room. Walt Digz, a renowned local DJ, wearing his signature blue and yellow Golden State Warriors flat-billed cap, spins the latest in Cuban music. The room is hot and crowded with sweaty dancers, eager to keep going as one song blends into the next. I put down my drink and ask Maribel to dance. Maribel, a charming, olive-skinned Spaniard with a smile that never seems to leave her, moves with ease and confidence as she mouths the words to the song. It may not be Havana, but I can imagine it when I hold her and we dance.

I first met her long ago at an outdoor concert. I remember saying, "You're a really good dancer. Where are you from?"

"Madrid," she said.

"Madrileña?"

"Yes," she said. "And you're Cuban."

I don't know if it was my accent or my dancing (maybe both), but I remember a surge of pride at her recognition of my history.

I feel the same when I go dancing at a place like the Boom-Boom Room on the corner of Fillmore and Geary Street. The dark bar flows along one side of the space to a stage at the back of the room. The funk and the deep bass vibrating my insides is the same music Connie and I danced to back in the late seventies. I no longer dance with reluctance but instead with satisfaction, because it's the music I grew up with, the music my neighborhood inspired. As on a night at Il Pirata, I look around and see a mixture of young and old vibing and moving like I am. The knowing looks recognize those of us who belong to another time, another place.

The lights dim. The lead singer looks out to the crowd that now claps and screams for the band to start. He taps the microphone.

"Is this on?" he says with a laugh. He turns back to the band and claps, "One. Two. One, two, three…"

The deep strike of the bass matches the drummer's beat, and the horns blast out the melody. I sip my rum. I snap my fingers to the music. I dance. And I dream, in a language of my own.

Eggs

Catherine C. Con

I

O N A CONVIVIAL small island, people visited each other frequently and unannounced. Someone would stroll in unexpectedly around meal time and be invited to join in the spread. If there was a pot of chicken and boiled eggs in this anise fragranced soy sauce broth, the host would just whip up a quick cucumber salad with garlic and chili oil; and dinner was quite adequate. This pot of juicy chicken with soft boiled eggs called for a whole chicken chopped into sixteen or so small pieces, with skin and bones, and twelve boiled eggs with runny yokes. The eggs were immersed in cold water in a pot on the stove top, the water brought to a gentle wavy boil. After four minutes, the eggs were spooned into water with ice cubes bobbing for another four minutes, cracked and peeled. The chicken pieces were sautéed in a deep pot in grapeseed oil to brown the skin, to render some fat; at that point, one part of soy sauce and nine parts of water were poured into the pot. The boiled eggs were also glided into this beautiful brown broth—whose surface gleamed with blotches of oil—along with a chunk of fresh ginger root, a palmful of star anises, one teaspoon of Sichuan pepper corn, and two tablespoons of rock sugar. This pot was then placed on a low fire and simmered for an hour and a half. For the sudden guest, a bowl of warm white rice, topped with a piece of the chicken, a boiled egg, and trickles of this fatty golden liquid over this small mound was served up. If this pot was empty when the guest sauntered in, a plate of easy over eggs glistening in peanut oil and salt crystals could be quickly pan fired and come to the rescue, and everyone would be happy.

My grandmother preferred a whole bulb of garlic instead of the chunk of ginger. The maid would always drizzle a table spoon of sesame oil over it before serving. My mother, who didn't spend much time in the kitchen, would ask for five fragrance powder. I grew up on the island savouring different versions of the chicken and boiled egg dish. When I left my home on the small island to come to America to further my study, I brought my recipes with me. I was a scrawny young woman with a hearty appetite for life. In the Cajun country, Baton Rouge, Louisiana, I attended Louisiana State University. I lived in the Lakeshore graduate women's dorm, a dorm surrounded by the two lakes on the edge of the campus. There were eight women on my wing. They were learned women, aloof, polite and distant. I ate my meals alone in the big kitchen, looked at the lakes and felt lonely. I was used to eating with friends and families. I had the island life in me. I made chicken and boiled eggs and invited all eight ladies to have dinner with me one Saturday evening. We became close, they showed me Mac and Cheese and other practical casserole dishes to survive the drudgery of study.

When spring came, one of my classmates invited me to her home for crawfish boils; I immediately fell in love with those spicy mud bugs. Her mother, a Cajun lady, educated me on Cajun seasoning. My small island life unbolted to cayenne pepper, smoky paprika, bay leaves, oregano and thyme. Not able to find star anise or Sichuan pepper corn in the only grocery store near the campus, I switched the flavoring for my chicken and boiled eggs to Cajun spices with Kikkoman soy sauce, Louisiana raw cane sugar and water. This chicken and boiled eggs became a fusion of Chinese and Cajun cooking. The heat of Cajun spices with a touch of the fragrance of soy sauce and a cooling light sweetness of the local cane sugar was magnificent. On Sunday afternoons, I often prepared a pot of chicken drum sticks and boiled eggs. I divided them into small packets of white rice, one drum stick, one egg and one serving of broccoli florets. These packets were wrapped in aluminum foils and stacked up on the shelves in the refrigerator with labels of my name on them. When I arrived in the dorm after a day of classes, study and lab, I unwrapped one packet and warmed it. In fifteen minutes, I fed my famished body, soul and spirit. Sometimes, a packet would be missing, and a five-dollar bill with a thank you note would be labelled with my name on it. This happened more frequently during the final exam week. I suspected Bonnie, the woman from Brooklyn, who was such a foodie, would try a packet here and there. Or maybe it was Malissa, who was getting a Food Science master's, and often spoke about adding my dishes to her class material. Or, whoever else was desperately hungry. There were sixty-two women in the graduate women's dorm, and it was difficult to detect who the grub burglar was.

II

I GOT MARRIED and had a girl. My family moved to Greenville, South Carolina. I continued cooking chicken with boiled eggs. I noticed my girl seemed to favor tomato sauce and ketchup, so I put toma-toes, ketchup, and some mustard in the broth instead of star anise or Sichuan pepper corn, or the Cajun spices, and the dish was well received. The chicken now tasted somewhat like a South Carolina BBQ chicken. This chicken and boiled egg dish had migrated with me, crossed the Pacific Ocean with me, and evolved with me, tinted by the local colors of the United States. Our next-door neighbor's little girl, Morgan, was in the same class with my daughter Eliza-beth. Morgan's parents worked and they did not come home till seven in the evening. She came over to do her homework with Eliz-abeth, and she didn't leave when I served dinner. She ate a lot of the boiled eggs in soy sauce with tomatoes, ketchup, mustard and sugar broth. The girls in the neighborhood organized an American Girls Club consisting of girls with different ethnicities in the surrounding houses. Morgan didn't want to be German, which was her inheri-tance, so Elizabeth made her an "Honorary Chinese Girl" badge. I think the tasty boiled eggs invoked her fantasy to be a Chinese girl.

III

I DON'T QUITE remember why I joined the track team when I was twelve. I ran some relays at track meets; I sat on the benches for most of the other races. We practiced after school, and I got home starving. Rice was ready and hot, sitting in the steamer waiting to be consumed for dinner; but everything else was raw. The maid, who had taken care of me since I was a baby, took one look at me and cracked an egg into a rice bowl. The egg yolk was marigold. She covered the egg with steaming hot rice, drizzled some soy sauce, sesame oil, stirred it all together and handed me the scorching rice bowl with white smoke. Each grain of the rice was wrapped in quivering egg juice tinted with brown soy sauce and emitting the scent of sesame oil.

"Be careful, it's hot." She said.

I didn't care if it burned my tongue. I hugged her and planted her sweaty cheeks with egg stained kisses after I had scraped the bowl clean. The taste of that egg-smothered rice, or rice-smothered egg, was impossible to forget.

I wanted to create that memory for my girl after her tennis practice. On our way home from the tennis court, I described this egg-rice dish.

"Oh, my, I'm hungry." She said.

I scanned the contents of my refrigerator in my mind: there were eggs, left over rice, and half a jar of Pace chunky Texas salsa. I was out of sesame oil and soy sauce, and there was not enough time to steam piping hot rice. How about "Huevo Ranchero?" I spread out the cold rice on a plate, dolloped salsa over the rice, cracked an egg over the salsa, and popped the plate in the microwave. In less than five minutes, I served up a plate of "Huevo Ranchero." She quietly consumed it, very satisfied. She had forgotten about the egg-rice dish I'd described with so much affection and nostalgia on our way home.

IV

NOT ONLY DID I have eggs in the afternoons after track practices, I had eggs in the mornings for breakfast as well. Sometimes not eggs from a hen, but eggs from mullet fish: a bowl of white rice topped with pieces of pan-fried mullet roe and some pickled turnips. I served my girl salmon roe on rice with a few drops of soy sauce for breakfasts sometimes until the breakfast menu was discussed in one of her kindergarten class and our salmon roe breakfast stirred up a little bit of a commotion. She came home that afternoon and protested, she didn't want salmon roe anymore, she didn't want to be eating different breakfasts from her classmates. I told her about Monkeys; Monkeys impersonated others. Poor child. I stopped serving Salmon roe on rice for breakfasts. Instead, I served cereal and milk, chicken eggs and bacon, and pancakes with Canadian maple syrup. Let her at least have the same breakfasts as the others. Let her be a little monkey for as long as she thought she needed to be.

Time flew by between eggs and roes. My little girl grew up, left home, and set up her own homestead. Just when I thought I was done with the adventures with eggs and roes, shrimp roes came to me in a mild May day on the Stockholm Archipelago. My husband and I, now empty nested, were in downtown Stockholm; number seven tram took us to Rosendals Tradgard which was "an oasis of growing and sustainability in the heart of Stockholm," according to the travel brochure. We got off at the last stop and walked the tree lined crushed stone paved path up to the garden café. Beds in wooden frames containing vegetables, flowers, and fruit trees adorned the road sides; ceaseless bird notes of the northern country twittered on the tree tops. The soothing sunshine and the caressing breeze were like sweet warm mulled wine that got me to the euphoria state effortlessly. Smoked shrimp was on the Special of the Day and I thought, yes, only smoked shrimp would do the honor of such a day. The smoked shrimp came in a slanted white bowl with a couple of slices of lemon and a cup of mayonnaise sitting next to an empty bowl for the shells. They were heads on, whole, about the size of my pinky finger. Each shrimp had a lump of shrimp roe between the head and the body. I sucked the roes and chewed the flavorful heads, then I peeled the tails and dipped them in the mayonnaise. The tails were tender and sweet, but the roes were incomparably luscious and delicate. I emptied my bowl of smoked shrimp, squeezed the lemon to clean my hands. Deep down inside me, a mysterious craving that was unknown to me was curiously satisfied. I sighed with content that my adventures with eggs and roes were not quite over yet.

I will not call my dad or my mother names x 19

Liwa Sun

And so you write with four pencils
at the same time. Tweak some strokes.
Do all the "I"s in one touch, vertical.
Margin them a bit differently. In this
note the joke prevails. You lose the
point, but who can blame you. Father
uses it to partition coffee and table.
Mother snatches in salvage and laminates.
Disproof by repetition, and the song grows tired.
Irreverent child is not cute anymore.

And you grow old. . . you grow old.

They stop glorifying sentimentality, and
the water comes to a boil. *Tough crowd,*
you say. They don't laugh. Should you be
coddled, or should you not? You drink ice
tea like a human. In the afterthoughts, you
live. Mom's door cannot hold you, or you are
just fat. One evening, curse words stop
signifying. You unfold the shopping receipts
and read them without sarcasm.

You become homeless long before
your parents' deaths.

Bazaar Bozorg

Mehdi M. Kashani

DURING HER PSEUDO-WEEKLY phone conversations with her parents, Zara never asked about Neda. Their mother, especially, imposed on Zara her sister's news. Through these unsolicited bursts of information, Zara learned that Neda had found a stint at Nokia's office in Tehran, Masoud had bought a Hyundai Elantra and Darya had formed her first full sentence. Zara could live with that much, random sporadic updates she received about her sister's family in the comfort of her studio apartment in Toronto, sufficiently far away. At least her parents had stopped asking for reconciliation.

Strangely enough though, even that trickle of news dried up for a few months—so much so that Zara ventured into checking Neda's Instagram, only to realize that it'd been deactivated. She continued resisting the urge to bring up her sister until one day, out of the blue, her mom asked, "Hasn't Neda been in touch with you lately?" to which Zara provided a hesitant no, prompting her mom's next question: "If she does, you'll talk to her, right?"

Zara did her best to sound neutral. "If it's an urgent matter."

Her mom's sigh bordered on relief, like she was appeased with Zara's answer, which meant something *urgent* was brewing. But to put things into perspective, a sense of urgency was Neda's norm.

THE NEXT MORNING, Zara opened her eyes to an email from her sister. Still in her nightdress, she powered through it with her groggy eyes, unblinking. It was courteous and concise, considering Neda's standards. It said that Neda and Masoud were getting a divorce (right on the first line, no prelude), that Masoud started to threaten he'd get custody of their daughter, that he might retract his claim if Zara asked him to, that he owed Zara big time. Then, the email ended with this line: *Can you come to Iran, Zahra? Please…*

Zara held the mobile in her hand as she jumped out of bed, turned on the kettle and peed in the bathroom. All that time, she scrolled through the short email, gazing at the words as if they could disappear any minute. *Divorce. Custody. Iran. Please.*

Even though she'd vocally wished for them to break up, it still came as a shock. The email was devoid of emotion, free of prolixity. It was as if a sponge had absorbed all the feelings and excess off the words, leaving only a bare foundation to build on later. And Neda's request at the end, whose idea was it?

Zara didn't respond. She was too shocked to dwell on an appropriate response. When she exited the internet-deprived subway near her office, her phone vibrated with a procession of alerts:

NEDA: Did you read my email? Let me know…

DAD: Zahra jan, see if you can help your sister. Do it for your mother?

MOM: Darya is our only grandchild. If you can save her, save her. I pray for you.

ALEX: Good morning Sexy.

Only the last message brought smile to Zara's lips. She replied: *can we meet tonight after work? Harbour Sq.?*

HARBOUR SQUARE PARK next to Jack Layton Ferry Terminal was the place that, three years ago, on their third date, Alex and Zara vowed exclusivity and sealed their first kiss. Since then, it had become their confessional place, where carrying cups of coffee, they talked about serious stuff. The last time they'd been here was a month ago, when Alex suggested they move in together and Zara refused.

Now, she was reciting the translated content of the email. Alex listened patiently, occasionally distracted by the passing of men and women with beautiful bodies in running gear.

When she was done, he pushed a lock of hair out of his face. That loose golden hair. "What an unexpected turn of events."

Alex knew the significance of this message. They were one year into their relationship when he asked why she wouldn't introduce him to her family. By then, she'd been to his parents' place in Hamilton a few times. So she told him everything about her life in Tehran, how she abandoned everything once Neda announced she was getting married.

Silence lingered on, almost slipping into an uncomfortable zone, until Alex noisily let air out of his mouth. "You think it's a good idea?"

She showed him her phone's display with dozens of unread messages. "Everyone in Tehran thinks so, it seems." She turned to him. "And you. What do *you* think?"

"Well, I do believe you'll need to end your self-imposed exile at some point. You can't go on like this, not visiting your parents, avoiding your country."

"But?"

He looked away from her. "I'm not too sure how that meeting with the man will go."

Not *your ex-fiancé*, not *your soon-to-be ex-brother-in-law*. The man.

"I doubt if such a meeting would ever take place," Zara said, but doubted her own words.

"It's not that I don't trust you. In fact, I'm not worried if the residue of some feeling suddenly pops out when you see him. The thing is you hate him so much that I'm worried about your mental health. I don't want you to come home an emotional wreck."

She was indeed an emotional wreck when she moved to Toronto and had continued to be one when she met Alex a year and a half later. She'd managed to hide much of it thanks to the space Alex gave her. That she was so used to her episodes of loneliness was the main reason she didn't agree to move in with him.

"It's funny, I always imagined your homecoming to be something I'd be a part of." He looked at her, studying her face. "Some other time, perhaps."

Three years into their relationship he was entitled to such fantasies. Nevertheless, Zara had resisted fantasies of her own. After what had transpired with Masoud, she was wary of labeling any relationship serious. That was the second reason she had said no to moving in with Alex.

She leaned over and kissed him, a quick peck on the lips. She didn't really have enough emotional resources to dwell on a future trip of the *hey-Mom-Dad-this-is-Alex* type. The one already in question made her stomach turn.

"I'll need more time to think it over," she said and once she did, she realized it was a vague answer. And Alex's faint smile didn't indicate if he knew what she meant.

She had meant to sleep on it, but when she arrived home, she saw another text from Neda: *As soon as the agencies open, I'll go and buy your ticket.*

The text was sent at 6:34 A.M. Tehran time and Zara knew her sister wasn't bluffing. She purchased a return ticket online and forwarded the confirmation to Neda with no salutation. Not even an FYI.

Even in light of the big favor Zara was going to undertake, owing her sister was something she could not stand.

IT WAS EASY to spot her parents in the crowd beyond the glass wall. Her dad was so tall and lanky he didn't even have to wave. Neda wasn't with them. She also had a remarkable height, was not to be missed. Only one of the few hereditary perks she'd usurped from their parents.

With her acquired polite Canadian manners, Zara cautiously navigated her cart forward. The exhausted passengers, eager to leave the drab carousel area with a possibly broken AC, kept pushing and elbowing her. She could've asked one of those uniformed guys to carry her luggage in exchange for a dollar or two. But she enjoyed her snail's pace, postponing whatever was about to happen behind those gates.

She wondered why Neda hadn't come. It wasn't like her, the drama queen, to spare the awkwardness of such a meeting under their parents' watch. She could be lurking somewhere in the bowels of the reception area, an idea that sent a chill down Zara's spine.

When she passed customs, as if caught in the orbit of filial affection, she thrust the cart forward more forcefully and it was then she saw a little girl standing between her parents. Her niece.

Unsure of how to receive Darya, Zara decided to buy some time by first hugging the adults. But no sooner did she throw herself in her mom's arms than she burst into tears. She then grabbed her dad and sniffed a few times until she managed to contain the flow. She'd never cried in her parents' presence for what had happened between her and Neda. Always too proud.

"And here is Darya," her mom introduced. "Couldn't wait till tomorrow."

Darya was holding a Sesame Street puppet—Bert or Ernie, Zara wasn't sure. She had Neda's eyes and Masoud's jaws, lucky to inherit either feature. She was the sole reason Zara stood there and her unawareness of her own centrality only doubled her innocence. "Oh, look at this beautiful lady. Aren't you supposed to be in bed?" Zara said through her sniffs.

Darya grinned, revealing two rows of incongruous milk teeth. "Mommy made an exception."

Zara was at a loss what to do or say. Seeking inspiration, she squinted around, surrounded by hugs and cries. No, not possible. She extended her hand. "Hi, I'm Zara."

"Come on Zahra," her dad protested. "Give your niece a hug like aunties do."

Maybe it was the magic of their embrace, or the delight in their faces that did it. Zara was amenable to fulfill any request to stretch that joyous moment. Still blinking to push the residue of tears away from her eyes, she bent over and hugged the girl.

THE NEXT DAY, Zara took a Snap downtown, all by herself. She was supposed to meet Neda to "strategize and maximize gains out of Masoud's guilty conscience." Zara had declined her sister's offer for a ride. She said she wanted to take a stroll before their appointment, which was true, if not the whole truth.

She arrived at *Haft-e-Tir* Square early enough. It was liberating to be by herself in the depths of the city she'd been raised in and been away from for six years. She walked down *Karim-Khan* Street, swinging by her favorite bookstores. Then she entered a handicraft shop. Back in Toronto, when she'd asked Alex what he wanted from Iran, he'd responded, "Just get me something handmade from *Bazaar Bozorg.*"

Alex had overheard the Persian name for the Grand Bazaar while Zara chatted with a friend. He'd taken special interest in the funny alliteration—the profusion of b's and z's. With only one week in Tehran, Zara knew she couldn't make time to go to the Grand Bazaar. Her parents were too crippled with arthritis to keep her company and they wouldn't let their precious daughter go alone. And she didn't want any of her local friends and family to learn about this trip—part of the deal she'd made. So, this store was possibly her only chance to buy something for Alex.

She found most of the merchandise gaudy, impractical or both. The few items she liked were expensive. The multitude of zeros in their prices made her dizzy. She had yet to catch up with the inflation. She'd check the price for a vase, and think she'd found a good bargain only to realize she'd missed a zero. She wandered aimlessly until her phone beeped: *Looking for a parking spot.*

THE COFFEE SHOP was Zara's choice. An impersonal setup, neutral ground to meet her sister. Café Kohan used to be one of Zara's favorites, coincidentally, one where she had never been with Masoud. She thought it would help, to meet Neda somewhere that didn't remind her of him. Only one other table was occupied, by two teenagers who recklessly kissed each other every few minutes.

Neda pushed the door open and her eyes glimmered. Her scarf was varying shades of red. Her light-brown coat fell just below her hips, which were held snugly in a pair of blue jeans. Still fashionable and tasteful with colors.

Zara placed her palms on the table, as if she needed them to rise. It was, she reminded herself, only a warmup before the fateful meeting with her ex. She'd better survive this one unscathed.

Neda shuffled in her direction, somehow weighed down by her

bag. "My big sister." Then, she stood opposite Zara, her chin level with Zara's beaky nose. "Am I allowed to hug my big sister or what?"

Zara nodded, wary of Neda making a scene. Those teenagers were staring already. Neda embraced her tight and Zara let the time pass. Once they sat down, Neda lifted the menu at an angle, seeing it without really looking.

"You know, lots of cool places opened since you left."

"I like here anyway."

"Of course, your comfort zone. How can I argue with that?" She raised a hand to stop Zara from protesting. "First, let's get things straight, okay? I understand you didn't come because of me. It was because of Mom and Dad, and maybe Darya. Charity for a girl you haven't met and probably aren't crazy about. That's that." She put the palms of her hand together and moved them to the right as if she was pushing that topic aside. "Ehsun, can I get a Café Glacé please?" she asked the bearded man who appeared with Zara's cappuccino. "As for me, I know you're gloating over my divorce. No, don't click your tongue and don't try to invalidate my claim. That's not the point. The point is I'm really thankful that you came all the way despite everything."

Neda was still good with words, blunt too. That was the first thing that occurred to Zara, even before verifying any of Neda's claims. "I was reading custody laws. They say the mother is given custody until the kid is seven."

"Yeah, Masoud knows people in court—"

"Mom said that too. But this is the clear text of law. Not a matter of dispute—"

"They don't know everything, Zahra."

Her voice suddenly turned poignant and Zara wondered if that was part of her performance. Something in Neda's purse beeped. She extracted her cellphone, covered in red like her outfit, and beamed at whatever appeared on the screen. Since when had her yellow-dominated taste in colors changed?

"Should I know what they don't know?" Zara asked, interrupting Neda's typing into her mobile.

"Masoud has some… things that might prove I'm not qualified for custody."

"Things as in evidence?"

"I'm not sure. My guess is some text messages and possibly pictures."

"What the hell, Neda! Did you do it again?"

"You know I'm not marriage material. And don't ask me why I got married in the first place."

"I was actually going to ask why you had a child."

Neda smirked. "Yeah, I wonder that too."

"So…" Zara waved in the direction of the phone. "That was what triggered your divorce."

"It was coming either way."

Zara sipped her cappuccino, not willing to offer a counterargument. Neda kept staring at her with a sly upturn at the corner of her mouth until Zara asked, "What?"

"Isn't it funny? We're living each other's lives. You were supposed to stay here. With them. Start a family. And me, I am the one meant to live abroad, to enjoy freedom, do whatever I want."

Like you aren't already doing whatever you want, Zara almost said. "I wonder whose fault it was."

"Why do you always have to look for the culprit? Why's everything so binary to you?" She pressed her forehead with the heel of her hand. "Sorry, I'm a bit edgy these days. So, how's Canada?"

"It's okay," Zara murmured.

"That's it? Gone for six years and *okay* is all you have to say? What about guys? Snatched any blue-eyed ones? You're blushing. Hey, I'm not going to steal him."

Zara had, in fact, prepared several ways of introducing Alex along with pictures. A summary for her parents with a plain mugshot. A more detailed one for Neda, and yet another one, glitzier with sensuous romantic pictures catering to Masoud. But now, she was taken aback by the casual manner with which Neda alluded to their history. Was cheating like any other grief that people could make fun of after an appropriate amount of time? But again, it was classic Neda. No moral compass.

"Despite your track record, that is." Zara tried to soften her sarcasm with a laugh.

"Or maybe because of. Oh Zahra, if only you could broaden

your world a little bit. You have your principles and you believe that I don't have any. Do you really think I didn't give a shit about you when that fiasco happened? I could never imagine, even in my wildest dreams, that I would fuck my only sister's fiancé. No, let me finish. And sorry about the language. You ask me why I had Darya? No, it wasn't a broken condom. When I got Masoud, I lost Mom and Dad. And you definitely. Then, I thought maybe if I got married, everyone would think how serious this whole business was, something beyond a mere whim. But that wasn't enough. I had to get pregnant. A baby would change it all, I told myself. A husband and a baby were the price I had to pay to pretend it was worth razing my sister's engagement to the ground."

"And it sort of worked. You won them back."

"But I lost you forever."

Neda's eyes flew over Zara's mouth. It remained slightly open, never wide enough to produce an *it-is-not-true*, simply because it was true.

"How about we stop talking about what you might have lost and start discussing what you want to attain?"

Neda frowned as if she'd forgotten the purpose of this meeting.

"Of course," she said before embarking on her spiel, during which Zara realized her sister had no *strategy*, only a volley of swearing and the desperate repetition of "He won't say no to you" and "You should catch him off guard."

BACK WHEN THEY were dating, they'd developed a routine: Zara would wait across the street from Masoud's office, occasionally holding some snack or drink in her hands, until Masoud emerged from the revolving doors. Apparently, Masoud was still in that gray cement building, only his office had risen from the fifth floor to the seventh.

The building had a heinous façade and Zara wondered if it'd always been like that. She stationed herself in the same spot, resisting the urge to remember her feelings the last time she was there. Employees began to trickle out. Some faces looked familiar. Masoud might have introduced them in the past. She wondered how he presented Neda to them later. Did he hide the fact that his wife and ex were sisters?

Masoud was now out, chitchatting with a man Zara didn't know. When they were about to part ways, Zara jaywalked the hazardous street, a skill she had reacquired after three days of trying.

He spotted her before she anticipated it. His eyes were skilled wanderers. Always on the lookout for interesting sights, peculiar cars, and unusually beautiful girls. He stepped forward and twisted his lips into a smile. If he was surprised, he had a good way of hiding it. In fact, Zara found herself more flustered, shoving her hands into her pockets to hide the sweat.

"In my daydreams, I always pictured you in a situation where I could hug you."

Over the past years, she'd led lengthy conversations with him in her head, random snippets of which now bubbled up like stubborn vomit heaving to throat only to retreat. "I'm sorry we don't live in your dreams."

"When did you come back?"

"Friday."

His small pupils swirled in his eyes as he did the math. "You must have missed me a lot then."

"Can we talk?"

"Yes, the obligatory talk. You hungry? There's a new pizza place a bit further in Shariati—"

"How about we go to your home and order delivery?"

She knew how shocking it would sound to him. Zara wasn't an easy girl, always so reluctant to step into his bachelor unit when they were dating. That was her upbringing, a virtuous girl, or so she thought even as her own sister—purportedly brought up by the same values—ended up snatching her husband-to-be. Zara always wondered whether her excessive chastity triggered their fallout, whether a dose of sluttiness was required to keep men around.

And no, she wasn't looking for makeup sex or to take revenge against her sister. Neither was she keen to show her bloomed recklessness. She simply was curious to see the life Masoud had prepared for Neda before things derailed, the life he would have prepared for Zara had things not derailed.

The silence stretched so long Zara feared he might say no. Ironic, considering she'd been the naysayer in their relationship.

"You'll find it a bit of a mess. But, what the hell," Masoud said, hailing a cab.

IT WAS A hell of a mess indeed. It took Zara some time to absorb the apartment. She sat on the edge of a rickety chair, exceptionally not covered in junk. Even though Masoud left most of the lights off, in the dim light, it was clear they stood amidst the ruins of his crumbling marriage.

Zara was more comfortable in her coat and scarf. She turned down Masoud's offer to hang them, which made him look both puzzled and hurt.

He shuffled towards the kitchen and opened the fridge. Zara made out the handle of a pan and the corners of some plates sticking out of the sink.

"Did she tell you she broke my heart?" He sighed at whatever he saw in the fridge, or at his own question perhaps. Now, Zara had a good opportunity to stare at Masoud without his staring back. He hunched his shoulders, a new development for sure.

She straightened her back. "She mentioned some evidence?"

"Evidence!" he snorted. "You must be glad in a way. We're even, in terms of broken hearts. Tie game."

Why was everyone worried about her settling scores? Did she come across as someone seeking a vendetta? Or, was it her archetype, easier for people to understand her?

"I don't compete with those who are dead to me." It came out harsh, yet she so enjoyed the aftertaste that she didn't take it back.

"No, you only visit their homes unannounced."

She was tempted to continue down this vein, emitting her accumulated hatred in spoonfuls of sarcasm. But no, that would be the wrong course of action. She pushed herself back, now leaning on the chair's back. "She wants custody."

His shoulders wobbled with laughter, a bit more than they should. "Oh God! She's exceptional. So manipulative. She convinced you to come all this way. You of all people."

"I had my reasons."

"She's recruiting everyone against me, even the grocery man across the street."

Zara's head was throbbing, could be the onset of a headache. "Let's talk about Darya."

Her request didn't alter his unfaltering gaze at the opposite wall. "With you, it all ended peacefully. But your sister. Oh my God. Everything is different. Chaotic."

Zara turned to the door that possibly led to the bedroom. It was obvious what Masoud was getting at, but she conjured up the familiar image: Neda riding Masoud with him crying out, *You are different, you are chaotic. You're a lovelier, sexier, better creature than Zahra.*

Masoud scuffled out of the kitchen. "Regardless of who she is, I should admit it was a smart move. She's well aware of my nagging conscience when it comes to you." He pushed away a few articles of clothing to make enough room on the sofa. "I'll do whatever you tell me to do. Give her custody and settle for the weekly visit."

He slumped onto the sofa. He was small, perhaps dwarfed by all the clutter. But still small. She'd probably grown accustomed to Alex's athletic physique. She wondered who would win if they ever wrestled. She chuckled inaudibly at the obvious outcome.

"Just think about Darya and her well-being," Masoud added, filling the silence Zara had been too distracted to fill.

"I don't really know her."

"But you do know your sister."

A *gabbeh* with sparse yellow designs hung from the wall behind him. A good and patient eye could still find tastefully decorated corners in that house.

"Children need their mothers Masoud, even if—"

She trailed off, unable to utter the words. How many times had she covered for Neda, all the way from breaking their cousin's toys to breaking her marriage vows? This sense of sisterly complicity!

"Not according to the Islamic laws of this country."

Masoud was always an avid champion of secularism, something that Zara was once worried would turn into a sore point with her religious parents. "Since when do you abide by Islamic laws?"

"I'm a worshipper in the temple of pragmatism."

"Which is another way of saying you're using Darya to get back at Neda."

"And we're back to where we started: my broken heart."

"You have a funny way of victimizing yourself in front of your biggest victim."

"You don't look like a victim to me. You live in the third best city in the world. You've become prettier. You look healthy. And I suppose you're with someone much better than me."

It was an invitation—bait perhaps—to spill out her private life. But her tongue was locked in her mouth. What was she going to tell him? That she picked Alex because he was a far cry from Masoud? That he was safe, that he was Canadian? Zara wasn't stupid. Canadians cheat too, but she'd numbed herself into believing he wouldn't. Alex was thousands of kilometers away from Masoud, spoke a different language, and had different diversions, hence he shouldn't cheat. It was like turning the pillow, hoping the cool side would never warm.

Masoud lurched forward. He knelt before her. The last time he'd done so was to propose to her. "Wanna hear my theory about why you came?" He shifted his weight. "You see in this whole thing an opportunity to mend fissures, now that I, the nuisance, am being kicked out of the scene. You came here to give Neda a second chance, to connect with your niece. You've always been the better sister. The forgiving one."

The big sister. The magnanimous sister. She'd heard these since she was little, and Masoud was the last person to remind. She was sweating under the layers of clothes she'd stubbornly refused to shed. And the heat alone wasn't to be blamed. There was something about the apartment. Its yellow cues. The disarray. The stuffed, stale air.

She rose with such force that the front legs of the chair jumped into the air. "I have to go."

He paced with her. "My offer is still valid. All you should do is ask. Speaking on your behalf, not anyone else's."

Down the hallway, his receding voice still reached her though the door: "You'll say, 'Masoud, I want you to give custody to Neda.'"

THE HOUSE WAS filled with a symphony of aromas. Saffron and turmeric. Cooked rice, vegetables and dried lime. Fried garlic and eggplant. Zara's mom was administering a bunch of pots and pans and her dad was setting plates on the dinner table. Five of them.

"Neda and Darya are on their way," her dad said, matter-of-factly.

Zara was expected to be the bearer of good news and this was a feast to celebrate her happy announcement. But, no one dared to ask her anything, not even Neda who later arrived with a Pyrex of *Sholeh-Zard* dessert and Darya in tow.

Darya was the only one perturbing the silence over dinner. One time when she addressed Zara, Neda intervened: "Darya, Auntie had a hard day. Stop bothering her."

And that was the only allusion anyone made to remind Zara she was on a mission. She tried to savor *Kashk-e-Bademjoon* and *Ghormeh-Sabzi*, not easy under the questioning gaze of their eyes. She knew how they felt, how it was to be anxious about some news, vacillating between wanting to know and not. All she had to do was to throw them a hint: *It went well*, or even, *What a nice day I had*. Finally, she raised her head, looking at no one in particular. "We'll talk about it later."

And that was it for the night. The next day, her father left early, and Neda dropped Darya off at their house on her way to work. Zara busied herself with the magazines on the coffee table. When she saw her mom's shadow hanging over the article she was perusing, Zara figured that her time was up, that her mom was resorting to one of those canonical mother-daughter moments.

Her mom continued to tower over her with a trembling chin, unsure how to proceed. At last, she beckoned at the room in which Darya was playing. "Take her out, somewhere. Anywhere. It's good for everybody." Her tone began like an order but wavered towards a plea.

It was a blessing in disguise, the best excuse to get out. Zara needed to talk to Alex, and not with her mom around. Alex was the only person she could dissect the situation with, a pair of foreign eyes. She took a moment to conceal her delight.

"Darya, get dressed," she shouted. "We're going to Bazaar Bozorg."

"No, not there," her mom protested. "I'll arrange for someone to go with you."

"Mom. I won't be alone." Zara nodded at Darya who was scampering to them now.

"We going shopping?" Darya asked, excited.

"Getting some souvenirs." Zara turned to her mom. "Can I borrow some money?"

ON THE SUBWAY, Zara took pleasure in observing people and their impossible dissonance. Within the same compartment she'd see women shrouded in black chadors along with ones in flamboyant coats and tight leggings. Young men with eyebrows plucked, next to bearded men reading Arabic prayer from worn-out books. At each stop, street vendors hopped on and off, offering a tapestry of unlikely objects: pens, notebooks, chargers, batteries, DVDs of *Harry Potter* and Iranian soap operas, slippers, candies—anything portable.

The path from the station to the Bazaar main entrance was short but swarmed with people and crisscrossed by narrow streets. Zara held Darya's hand firmly as they zigzagged through the incessant hum of cars and motorcycles with coughing exhaust pipes, hucksters advertising their bric-a-bracs, pedestrians darting across always chatting, usually in disagreement, and in total disregard of adding to the constant noise pollution.

Zara tried calling Alex a couple times. No response. She bought Darya an ice cream, hoping Alex would call her back while Darya was busy licking. They sat on the sill around a dried water fountain and Darya placed her stuffed toy on her lap. Zara squeezed the puppet's red nose. "So, which one is this guy? Bert or Ernie?"

"How do I know? You posted it for my birthday."

"Did I? You're lying," Zara said, shrill in mock accusation. "So, tell me. What else have I bought for you?"

Darya craned her neck and jutted out her lips in a gesture of thought. "Lego... Mademoiselle Kitty. And Nani, but Diba broke it so she stopped talking."

"I'm sorry I missed your birthday parties."

"Diba's cousins in *Amrika* Facetimed with her on her birthday."

Zara didn't know what sort of excuse would work on a five-year-old, so she went for the easiest: "Sorry honey, I was so busy."

"Mommy said you were mad at her."

"She said that? What else did she say?"

Darya looked at her, her nose and mouth behind her vanilla ice cream. "Mommy also said that you left Iran because she did something nasty."

"Well, that was in the past, before you were born," Zara said as if the mere chronology of events made them irrelevant.

"She's done it again. That's why Dad is divorcing her."

Darya's parents, Zara knew, had anger issues. They both had to win an argument at any cost. That their child was in their earshot wasn't of much importance.

"Darya jan, the adult world is a complex one, especially that of husbands and wives."

"Do you have a husband?"

"I do not. But... I do have a boyfriend. Do you want to see him?"

She thumbed the gallery on her mobile and passed it to Darya. "His name is Alex and it's going to be our little secret."

Darya began to swipe pictures around. Zara knew enough not to trust Darya's secrecy. In due time everyone would know about Alex. They would learn Zara danced with him in a backless dress, that he was kissing her cheek, that they strolled towards the camera in swimsuits during a bright sunset. It all felt fine now, filtered through the innocence of a child.

"Does he speak Canadian?"

"English. And French."

"I know English. I can count to fifty."

"I didn't know you could count in any language."

A message popped on the screen, over the pictures Darya was absentmindedly browsing: *Good morning sexy!*

Zara blushed, though Darya couldn't possibly read. Zara gently seized the phone from her niece and called Alex, their first contact since her arrival. After a few rings, he appeared on the screen, lit from his left and in a gray undershirt. Zara held the phone at arm's length to fit Darya in the frame. She squeezed Darya's shoulder to inch her towards the camera. "Look who is here. This is Darya."

She talked rather loudly to overcome the noise around them.

A few heads turned. Talking in English was not something peo-ple were used to in that traditional neighborhood. Waving at Alex, Darya emitted a discreet *hello*.

"*Chetori?*" Alex enunciated.

"I'm fine, thanks," Darya recited in fluent English.

"Wow, we have an English speaker here," Alex said. "Where's everyone else?"

It was a loaded question. Who else was privy to their relation-ship?

"Just me and Darya. We're in Bazaar Bozorg!" She tilted her phone sideways to give him a panoramic tour. When she looked at the screen again, Neda was calling. Zara rejected the call.

"I missed out big time," Alex said. "Will tag along next time."

"He says he wants to visit Iran with me. What should I tell him?" Zara asked Darya, dialing up the mischief in her voice.

Darya grabbed the phone and drew it close to her face. "I take you to bazaar."

Zara brought the phone close. "Now, since you're a good boy, we are going to buy you some gifts."

The image froze for a moment, portending a connection failure, and when it came back Alex said, "I miss you baby."

The screen was replaced by a call notification with Masoud's name. Zara pressed the reject button, letting Alex fill the screen again.

"I miss you too," she said.

A truck honked so loud Alex winced on the other side of the world. "What did you say?"

"I thought you were good at lip-reading," Zara said.

Alex was silent. Either he didn't like her smartass answer or, worse, the connection was dying.

Zara pressed the phone harder. "I said I miss you."

But Alex was gone.

"I was telling him I missed him," she said.

"I know," Darya said.

"What should we do now?"

Darya was working on the disintegrating wafer. "Buy him a pres-ent?"

The sun was beating down on them. Zara and Darya were the only people sitting. Everything and everyone were whirling around them like in a Disney musical. Zara dropped the phone in her purse. Calling Darya's worried parents could wait. They could scramble through a brief limbo while Zara was having some quality time with her niece. She stood and slapped her backside to clear the dirt. She clenched Darya's hand, sticky with the melted gelato, and together, they merged with the people entering the domed tunnel of the bazaar.

DEAD WORSHIP

Chekwube Danladi

I ask that you deify your evenings   or form a new theory of antimemory
        where each new doing means to   counter what was left to recall, looping
over and over in the name of new self-conduct rules (such as: don't spend night
        more than twice a week) or forsake   all the blood that vacates as traitor,
abandoner. To think more seriously of   taking your mama's advice and bringing in
        your dry clothes, your shoes,   since   when left out for the night, no spirit will wonder
where you are but will come direct   to your door   knocking
        will call out to you by name: *chekwubeolisa*   *I am your antecedent*
Come now to guide you home.   Saved from a new taboo.
        So advised to thank the darkened   realm, granting your continued transit
every time lumbering to bed from else–   where or elsewho. To have
        used so much another body   for passage and have forgotten to
commemorate the proto-memory.   *Pssst.*   So call it out by the angle of the dark hour.
    Ekwensu is also called the god of bargains, which is why he colors the night black.

Moon Egg

Sergio Aguilar Rivera

THE LITTLE ONES appeared after I gave birth. But before they appeared and before I gave birth, I had been sleeping in the hen house. I remember one of those late nights very well. Big hand on the 3 small one between the 6 and 7, still awake and sitting behind an old desk, a clutter of flashcards and dictionaries in front of me. My old Luxo lamp provided the only light. I didn't have much to do during my late pregnancy except eat and dread the birth, so I tried to distract myself by charting the etymological origins of certain words, how their metaphorical and rhetorical meanings changed through time. I created a chart for the word *sun* and then *god* (both of which produce fairly crooked word trees).

Justice seemed like a natural progression. I learned that *justice* comes from the Latin *iustus* which, at its most basic, means *upright*. The Old French is spelled the same way although probably pronounced differently. The encyclopedia gave mention of the Sumerian god Utu, god of the sun and of justice. I laughed at how perfect and unified it all seemed.

After jotting down some of the info on the flashcard, I tried to fall asleep but was unable to. I attributed my insomnia to the cold, although now I realize it probably wasn't the cold, and if it was, it was a cold of a different kind, a cold divorced from sense. I put on my robe and pink slippers and grabbed my pillow. I stepped out to a dark hallway. My eyes widened. I was seven months pregnant, and my belly was so big and heavy I had to press my hand against my vertebrae to keep my back in place. It was an exhilarating thing to walk through the dark, skulking down the narrow hallway. I guided myself in the dark by running my hand across the smooth of the daffodil wallpaper. The sound of my fingers scraping. Eventually, I reached wood which meant I had reached the door of the apartment after mine. By the time I got to the end of the hallway, my eyes had adjusted enough to the dark that I could more or less see my surroundings: cockroaches scuttling across the linoleum, a teddy bear head separated from its body and all the fluff on the floor.

I went up the stairs that led to the rooftop, one step at a time. I reached the top, but my breath was heavy; before I opened the door that gave way to the outside I took a deep breath.

I turned the rusty knob, practically had to kick the door open. I half expected to see the moon, but there was none. Expected to see the stars, but no. What I did see was the tawny glow of the city underneath rising up, blending colors with the dense clouds, like an old shellac varnished upon the sky.

The landlady, Doña Maru, kept a henhouse up there, tucked in the corner of the flat roof. Doña Maru only rented out her rooms to women, usually young women, and usually women with nowhere to go. She kept the hens so that we'd always have something to eat. "These eggs are yours for the taking," I remember she said when I moved in.

I walked towards the coop, following the hum of the sleeping hens. Even before I stepped inside the hen house, I could feel the heat emanating outwards from within. I unlatched the door to the coop and walked in. The hens stirred a little. A brooding hen is a wonderfully warm creature. I dropped my pillow down on the floor and plopped myself down, could barely squeeze in but I did. Sitting there was like being under heated water, so lovely that I felt enclosed in an egg myself.

A heating bulb gave the hens a scorched glow. I hoped they didn't mind my being there, stealing their heat. Maybe they thought, "you not only eat our eggs but you also eat our warmth. You are monstrous." But part of me wanted to believe they liked me being there. I put hands on my belly, ran my hand across, sternum to navel. I planted my palms on the fleshy slope, kept them there waiting for some movement. The baby inside me had stretched my skin quite violently, stretch marks streaking the sides of me, like red rivulets. I traced the markings with my fingers, traced them from memory since I couldn't quite see them in the dark.

I tried falling asleep and I almost accomplished this had it not been for a strange sound I heard, a cooing that was rough and loud, more so than what I was accustomed to from the hens. I waited for a moment both hoping and dreading to hear the sound again, and it wasn't long before I heard it. It took me some time before I could figure out what it was. It was the rooster. I had forgotten about him. He was above me, resting on a shelf just below the aluminum ceiling. He was there to fertilize the hens, introduced by Doña Maru two days before because she wanted more chickens. Something about the way he hummed caused me unease but eventually, I found sleep.

I woke up to the sound of the rooster's call, several magnitudes too loud. He sang on top of my belly, looking straight at me while he crowed. His feathers caught shine from the morning light, and the green on his breast became emerald and the orange something close to fire. I felt worthless beneath this bird, black beads for eyes, as if it could stare all the way through me. Doña Maru had often railed against the pride of roosters, "how proud the rooster to think it's worthy of announcing the sunrise" she'd say. It clutched its talons on my stomach. I had to smack it away to brush it off.

LILY WAS BORN at night. I remember the fat moon shining outside the window while I heaved and heaved as if to expel my soul.

Doña Maru brought me home from the hospital. When she opened the door to my room, I was greeted by an unbearable smell of lilies. "They're pollen free," she assured me with a smile. Doña Maru remained and washed my dishes despite my insistence that she'd done enough for me. I dropped to my bed exhausted, holding my child.

She looked like a white clump of clay waiting for a bolt of lightning to spark her up. I thought to myself, I'm not ready for this, and my eyes welled up although I didn't allow them to shed. I didn't tell Doña Maru that Lily had emerged dead silent, her eyes clammed up, and that the doctor had to hit her twice on the behind to get her to cry. The sound that spouted from her mouth was something I was sure I had never heard before, but from what realm it came I could not say.

Lily did not take from my breast easily. Her lips clamped onto my nipple only a brief moment then spat white liquid onto my skin and began to cry, hot scarlet rising up her throat and spreading across her pudgy face. I encouraged her, tried to modulate my voice into something that might be considered pleasant, but she cried even louder as if offended by my efforts. I bobbed her in my arms, up and down, up and down, the obvious pattern, her cry rising and falling like a yoyo. And soon, it was not just she who was crying but I as well. I offered her my breast again, but she reeled back and cried even louder. I wondered if something was wrong with my milk and remembered what the doctor had said about a protein-rich diet. Maybe my milk lacked potency.

The apartment building had a name: La Choza. It housed thirty-five women. The only man to step foot inside was the mailman, a pervy fellow who always slipped love letters through our door slits. It was common for some of the residents to get together and read the letters out loud to each other, laughing at the mailman's obscene suggestions and ludicrous pining. The women thought me shy as I seldom joined in their merrymaking. In fact, none of the girls knew I was pregnant until I began to show. Still, they each paid me a visit after her birth and even brought me plates of food.

TWO WEEKS AFTER Lily's birth, I made the effort up to the rooftop, greeted the hens whom I hadn't seen since being taken to the hospital. The rooster strutted towards me. I kept my distance from him. His eyes were black amongst his red wattle and comb. He flapped his wings as if to warn me of something, but then chased after me flashing his talons. I grabbed a broom and kept him at a distance, but he persisted and managed to pierce my leg with his spur. I locked myself in the coop. He sprung on the wiring, his talons sharp and reddened with my blood. There was mania in that bird. He finally quit after me and flung himself toward a pair of pigeons perched on the hip-high wall surrounding the edge of the roof. The pigeons spread their wings and flew off and the rooster stood in their spot as if victorious.

I grabbed three eggs from underneath one of the hens and sneaked past the rooster, downstairs to my room. Sticky blood wet on my jeans. The gash was small but deep.

Lily's cry echoed in the hallway as I walked through it.

Once in the kitchen, I turned the knob on the stove to meet the ignition arrow. The spark caught the gas, a blue flame spread out like a wave and shrunk into the usual flower shape. I cracked open an egg and let its contents land on the skillet.

That's when the first little one emerged. That was the first egg.

The thing was me, or something resembling me. It was the size of a stick of butter and I only use that as a comparison because I remember the stick of butter sitting on the counter by the stove. It was naked and her head disproportionately large, and it had a giant smile that seemed frozen in time, exposing all her dentures. It just lay there in the pool of yolk and butter, its eyes affixed on the ceiling. I nearly purged myself, had to hold my mouth with my hand. I tottered backwards, hit the wall behind me, and slid down until my ass touched the floor. I didn't dare look back into the skillet. My mind was somewhere else and I only came back to the moment when I perceived a sizzle from the skillet. The little one climbed out of the edge of the skillet, her eyes tortured but her smile still there. She ran around in circles on the stove top, her tiny body releasing just a bit of smoke. She finally jumped off to the tiled floor. I pulled my feet back and watched as it scurried this way and that, behind the garbage can, under my fruit table and finally crawling under the fridge. Then I heard Lily cry.

I ran to my daughter and brought her into my arms. She quivered but I held on to her regardless. I paced around the room trying to get my head straight.

I tried to explain to myself what I had seen but couldn't. That thing was me, or some version of me. I felt guilty. I didn't know why I felt that way. I felt shame, having a little thing like that running around my apartment, that little thing of me hiding under my fridge. The world didn't need more of me, not in any form, how could it.

I glanced over at the desk where the flashcards with *sun, god,* and *justice* still lay. The Luxo lamp shone on the words. I stared at the flashcards, repeating the words to myself. *Sun, God, Justice.* Over and over, I said the words until they stopped being words, just sound from my mouth. And then I saw a scurry, like some insect but it wasn't an insect. It was the little one. She approached the flashcards with her giant smile, shuffling towards them in tiny steps. The light shone above her like a celestial beam. She kneeled before the cards. She stared at each one, stamped her feet on them. She turned to face me. Her eyes were black beads. She lifted all the three cards from the desktop and ran off with them, jumping into the crevice behind the desk.

I barely slept that night, my ear pricked to every sound in the room, wondering where the little one ended up. Lily began to cry at some point which I welcomed as it cut the pervasive silence of the night, gave me some reprieve, a distraction. I took her to the wicker chair next to the window and we rocked back and forth under the moonlight. I tried to distract myself. I thought of words. *Sun* from the Old English *sunne. Heaven* from the Proto-Germanic *hibin,* a covering, a place of bliss. *Coil, Dragon, Saint.* Words are like eye holes to different rooms. I look into the eyehole and see what's inside. My life. Her life.

I sat there with these dizzy thoughts. I dreaded to see the sunlight, I dreaded to hear the rooster crow. But as always, the sun did rise and the rooster did crow.

THE NEXT MORNING, I found the two other eggs I had brought down were cracked, yellow yolk smeared across the counter. They reeked. I wiped the counters down with bleach. I forced myself upstairs to the roof again. The rooster crowed when it saw me. Doña Maru was up there, hanging laundry on the clothing lines webbed across. She had a cigarette hanging in her mouth as was her custom. She was a large woman with arms that looked like mudslides. She laughed at the rooster, "I think this rooster thinks you're the sun!" She then saw my face and her smile inverted and she asked what was wrong.

"I think I ruined the eggs."

I told her about what had happened the night before. She nodded, stroking my head for comfort.

We went inside the hen house and the first thing we noticed were the green flies buzzing around as if in a frenzy. The hens flung themselves out of the enclosure as soon as we opened it. The same sour, dead scent. Most of the eggs were cracked. Pinching her nose with her fingers, Doña Maru cracked one of the uncracked eggs with her spare hand. Out came the thing, all smeared by that awful smelling yolk. Doña Maru did something I would have never done. She grabbed it. She brought the thing close to her face, inspecting it, turning it over in her palm. Soon it began to move and it wrestled against her and at some point even bit into the web between her fingers. Doña Maru didn't flinch. "She's you," she said. I felt awful hearing her say that, confirming what I had suspected but wished was not true. She closed her palm upon the thing, pressed her fist with all her might, pressed and pressed until her veins began to pop. When she finally opened her fist, the thing was motionless, probably dead.

"We'll find them," Doña Maru assured me.

The next morning, we burned every egg the chickens laid before the little ones could hatch. We reasoned that at most, there were ten little ones running around the apartment building. We knew they were inside the building because they made their presence known. They seemed to be running through the ventilation as I could hear the pitter patter of their steps, coming and going, and when I turned on the heat I was greeted by a terrible pestilence.

They not only spoiled the air but my food as well. They stole crumbs of food left over during the night, going so far as to take my bananas which caused me great anger as they were my only source of potassium. I decided to clean my apartment as thoroughly as I could. I took out all the dishes, silverware, cooking ware from the kitchen cabinets and sprayed everything with bleach. When I opened the cabinet under the sink, I found three of the little ones eating the fuzzy mold spreading in the back. They scurried as soon as I tried to spray them with pesticide.

The other women in the building complained about the scent and soon they had more things to complain about as the little ones got into the wiring and plunged the building into darkness. Doña Maru gave us all candles, said she'd have an electrician over as soon as possible. But before that, she had the building fumigated. We had to disoccupy our rooms to avoid the fumes so Doña Maru decided we should all sleep upstairs. She laid out a number of mattresses and tied some hammocks to the poles that held up the clothing lines. I took one of the hammocks so that I could sway with Lily, maybe help her find sleep that night.

The others obviously blamed me for their inconvenience, for invading their homes with pest. "It makes sense that it'd be her. She's always coming and going, she was bound to bring in some filth at some point," I heard one of the women say. They questioned the way I was raising my child, remarked on how small and skinny she was, chided me for being a bad mother, too young to be responsible. I ignored them as much as I could, didn't give them the pleasure of seeing me cry.

That night on the rooftop, I peered into the hen house and saw the hens climbing up to their shelves. Doña Maru had once told me they slept high off the ground to avoid rats. Above them was the rooster. He looked at me with those black beads he had for eyes. He bobbed his head up and down. That rooster made me sick with fear. I blamed him for the little ones. "You got bad eyes," I said to him. I remember wanting to wring his neck.

I turned away from the hen house and lay down on the hammock with Lily, swaying back and forth to lull her into sleep. I wondered whether it was a bad thing for her to be exposed to the outside air. The moon was out, looked like a clipped fingernail. Perhaps due to Lily's calm or to the fact that I felt safe from the little ones, my head was clear enough to think about the word *justice*. I spoke the word out loud, which brought to mind the sun, God, and then even the rooster came to mind. It brought to mind a circle, then a beam of light shooting upwards, the vertical. I tried to drop myself as far into the word as I could, to think about it independently, but the word could only exist in relation to these other elements. I said it over and over again under my breath. At some point I wondered whether justice had ever been associated with the moon.

THE FUMIGATION WAS not much of a success. We found one dead. Its body lay inside a cereal bowl sitting on my neighbor's sink. She threw the tiny body into the trash heap in the alley. The others we assumed were alive because we could still hear their frenetic steps in the space between the walls.

I saw one give birth a few days after the fumigation. It happened inside my fruit basket. A little one lay by herself on top of a banana, her whole body covered by sunlight. Her face was red and her belly huge, proportionately speaking. She didn't make a sound of course as it seemed they were incapable of that. She pushed and pushed and soon came out a thing. She was not a baby but another little one, maybe a third the size of the original. She came out slimy and smelly, and soon she was running around wild, climbing on top of the bananas and the apples. It reached the rim of the basket and leapt out. The "mother" was up and running herself a few minutes later. I threw the fruit out. They could multiply. I hadn't thought about the possibility—but they could multiply. I thought about more versions of me running around. And what if the daughters could have their own daughters, and their daughters could have their own daughters, becoming smaller and smaller until reaching the microscopic, and then even smaller than the microscopic. Me all over atoms. It was too much to handle, my head ached. My heart pounded and pounded, pumping blood and adrenaline all over so that I had a hard time keeping my breath under control. I lay myself down, counting one two three four to calm myself but the counting only ramped up my fear as it reminded me of the little ones multiplying.

My legs were wobbly, my head felt heavy. But above all I was tired, tired of being fearful and guilty, tired from waking up every night to Lily's crying, tired of hearing the women in the building berating me. What did anyone truly know about me? I asked myself. The answer was nothing. I looked at Lily sleeping to the side of me in her crib. I looked at her face, all compressed by sleep, how her nostrils trembled. Every now and then, she sucked in more air than usual and her whole body shook and then relaxed. The longer I looked at her face, the less of a face it became, and instead became, what? Maybe a portal to sleep. Perhaps. I fell asleep easy that night despite the discovery of multiplication.

THE NEXT DAY around 2:30pm, when the lethargy of day hits hard, I felt something strange in my bones, a kind of cold similar to the cold I felt when pregnant with Lily. I wondered why I felt cold. It was summer and the days were hot, so it didn't make much sense. I stepped outside my room and went down to the lobby. Doña Maru sat there with a fat cigar in her mouth, watching a soccer game. "You look awful," she said to me, smiling big. She took Lily from my arms and goo gooed at her. "I haven't seen the mailman in a while," she said offhandedly. "That man made me uncomfortable," I said. "I get that. Seemed like the demon of lust himself. I've been trying to get a new mailman for years now, but you know how the world is."

It was three days later that we found the mailman dead in a closet where Doña Maru kept her cleaning supplies, his body torn to bits. He was riddled with little ones, eating from his flesh. A great feast for them. The residents laughed seeing the mangled body. "Your little ones ate the pervy mailman," one of them said to me. "Isn't that a relief."

I WENT BACK to sleep inside the coop, this time with Lily. She did not cry in the coop. I think it was the warmth, or maybe something else, I don't know. But I found relief there from her crying. She grabbed my face and laughed. The hens slept above me. I thought about the mailman, his habit of staring at us with those eyes that never seemed to close, ruddy cheeks as if he were forever drunk. The little ones ate him. No more mailman delivering love letters. I smiled and fawned. I stared at the rooster high above me, occupying saints' space. "You are the devil," I said to him. "Just like our mailman."

I killed the rooster before it could sing the sun. My hand reached out to his head and clamped on. I twirled and twirled his body like a top. He was stiff and then loose. The body fell to the floor, but I kept the head in my hand, the blood dripping from my fingernails. Never have I felt the kind of relief I felt that night, seeing that bird's head separate from his body. I plucked his feathers until he was all bare. I gutted him. I cleaved his body into pieces. And then I ate him in a stew.

AFTER I KILLED the rooster, the little ones quelled. Eventually, I learned to live with them. I left food out for them which they gladly took. They seemed to enjoy the rotten stuff, old spinach, spoiled cheese. They never bothered Lily. I never again saw them during the day, except once. It happened during a solar eclipse. The moon covered the sun and plunged my part of the world in darkness. I could see how the birds perched on their trees thinking it was night. The little ones emerged from inside the walls. Many of them were pregnant. One of them, one of the larger ones, carried some flashcards. She was the first, the original. This I knew by the burn marks on her back, from the time she burned in the skillet. She carried the words *sun*, *god*, and *justice*. She dropped them next to my feet. Lily could crawl. She laughed seeing all those little things about the floor and she chased after them. They avoided her, running around with their big smiles, their teeth chattering like those windup gag toys.

I picked up the flashcard and saw that it was worn out and dirty, the writing on it barely legible. Then I saw how they climbed up my desk, little ones of all sizes. There must have been thousands of them. The bigger ones spaced themselves out on the desk while the smaller ones filled the space between them. I could see the eclipse through the window. Eventually, they formed something that looked like a pattern. I tried to discern what it was. The pattern shifted, moved, seemed alive. Looking at that pattern, I thought about language, I thought about the moon, I thought about multiplication, I thought about God. The god I thought of is small like these little ones, exists infinitely small, does not look down from above but looks from within.

I picked Lily up from the floor. She giggled. Her cheeks were fat now which caused me tremendous happiness. I looked at the eclipse, waning, the sun returning to claim its spot. But during those seven minutes when the moon covered the sun, I believed that the God of Justice was also the God of the Moon. And not a god, but a goddess.

MY CLEANING AWAY

Josey Foo

My cleaning away clutter with the sweep of my arm.
My incredibly difficult own thoughts.
I don't imagine this humming in my ears has meaning.
What am I missing?

No one's strong belief makes me possible.
I don't imagine the thousand leaves underfoot and in the shadows
    of trees
hear, see, are other than indifferent to me.

I've been feeling now a long time
sensations making completely indifferent consequential sensations.

I've begun not being involved
in the grander scheme of things.

KOREAN JESUS

Pete Hsu

I. Call to Worship

WHEN I FINALLY find Korean Jesus, I can tell who he is right away. I can tell he's Korean because of his face and also because of his accent, but the Jesus part I don't get until after listening to him preach for a while.

It's late summer, Tuesday night, early evening, Central Park, Pasadena, California. It's hot. The hottest day of the year so far. It's looking to stay hot all night. I'm hot. I'm standing in the sun. I'm wearing long pants and a sportscoat. I have the coat on for fashion, but also because I've got something under my coat that I don't want anybody else to see. Jesus is in the sun too. It doesn't look like the heat is bothering him. He's sitting at a concrete park bench. It's not really a bench but more like a picnic table. It's a picnic table with benches connected to it. Two benches connected to it, one on each side.

There are twenty, twenty-one people with him, mostly white, or actually about fifty-fifty white and Asian. Most of them are standing. Six are sitting at the table with Jesus. They're all young. Except for Jesus. Jesus looks older, like 30-something or forty even. Older than me, and I'm already older than most of the crowd here. Most of the crowd here looks young. They're dressed in what looks like beachwear: Board shorts and swimsuit tops or tank tops, sunglasses, visors, stuff like that. Some of the men not even wearing a shirt. Jesus is sitting in the middle of everyone. He's preaching. It's like a monologue. Like he's giving a lecture, but casual.

Jesus says: This all starts when you're little, like really little, too little to understand consequences.

Somebody says: How old?

Some other people laugh when that person yells out, how old. Jesus laughs too.

Jesus says: How old? Oh dang. Come on. I mean, I don't know. It's not like a specific number. It's just little.

Jesus puts his hand out in front of himself to sort of show how tall of a kid he's talking about. The people around the table nod.

Jesus says: When you're still little like that, we come around to each of you and ask you what you want. And whatever it is you wish for right then, we do it.

The people around the table laugh.

Jesus says: I'm being serious here, you guys. Totally serious. Every kid, when they're little, gets one wish, and whatever that wish is, we grant it. And I mean whatever it is. Anything. Whatever it is that they want right then.

The people around the table laugh again. Jesus laughs too. But it's not the kind of laugh to show that he's just joking around. It's the kind of laugh to show how this whole thing could potentially get really fucked up.

Jesus says: You can probably guess what something like 80% of the wishes are.

Somebody says: Candy.

Somebody else says: Toys.

A third person says: Puppies.

Jesus says: Puppies? Who said puppies?

The person who said puppies raises her hand. Jesus gets up halfway from his seat and reaches out his hand. The person who said puppies doesn't seem to know what he wants. Jesus motions for her to come closer. She comes closer. Then Jesus gives her a hard high-five. The high-five makes a loud slap sound. The person who said puppies rubs her hand like it really stings.

Jesus says: There you go! Puppies! Little kids love puppies. Fluffy, downy, googly-eyed puppies. Who can blame them. Right? Can I get an amen?

Everybody says amen. Even I say amen. Everyone says amen right away except for this guy next to me. He doesn't say amen right away. Then he suddenly says amen after everybody else says amen. It just comes out. It's awkward and real loud. The people around him look at him like they're mad or judgmental, or maybe just surprised.

Without thinking too much about it, I reach out and pat the guy who didn't say amen on the back, like a friendly pat. A chummy pat. Like how you'd pat somebody on the back to show them that you appreciate them, like they'd just done something that you appreciate. He sort of drops his head a little bit and smiles as if to show me that he appreciates me too, that he appreciates the pat on the back. Then Jesus goes on.

Jesus says: So, all those 80% of wishes. Let's call them puppy-wishes. All those puppy-wishes, we just go ahead and do it. We don't even think about it, we just go ahead and do it. But...

Then Jesus pauses and looks around. It's almost 8PM but it's still 100 degrees out, maybe more. It's still light out too. Mostly light. Just a little bit dark. Jesus can see everybody. Everybody can see everybody else. We can all see Jesus.

Jesus says: It's the other 20% though. That's when things get sketchy. Because we still have to grant their wishes. Whatever it is. Even if it's, excuse my French, but even if it's really jacked up. We still do it.

Some of the people gasp out loud like they're cartoon characters. I laugh. Then pretty fast I stop laughing because I realize they're not being sarcastic. They're really gasping because this is really scary to them.

Jesus says: Yeah. You know it. I mean, sometimes these little kids, bless their hearts, they don't know any better. How can they? That's the whole point. If they knew better, it'd be too late to give them their wishes. So, they don't. They don't know any better.

The crowd starts shifting around and grumbling. Some of them are whispering to each other under their breath like muttering. Jesus raises his hands like to have everybody settle down.

Jesus says: Okay, okay. Don't freak out. Don't let your imaginations get carried away. It's not some kind of sociopathic stuff. It's not kids wishing for people dead! Come on! Is that what you guys are thinking? Little kids wishing their dads or baby brothers to drop dead or their moms or their teachers? No!

There's a kind of collective sigh of relief. Then there's a little bit more rumbling. People are getting restless. They're probably getting restless because this thing is going kind of long and also, it's just so hot out. I shift around. I'm sweating all over. I wipe my forehead with my coat sleeve. I pull at my waistband. My waistband is especially uncomfortable and sweaty because I've got a gun tucked in there. I want to take the gun out, but I can't because I don't want to alarm anybody. So, I leave the gun there. But it's not comfortable at all.

Jesus says: No, no, no, I mean, I'm just saying, there's some bad people out there. I sometimes wish these kids would just go ahead and wish them dead. But they don't. They're still little. Too little for justice, unfortunately. And you get it, right? I say unfortunately because it'd really make everybody's life a lot easier if we could just get rid of a bunch of the bad guys right then and there. You know what I mean?

Some people nod in agreement. I don't nod because I'm not really sure I agree. It might seem like I would agree or that I should agree, and it's not that I disagree. I just don't know for sure if I agree.

Jesus lets us all think about this for a couple more seconds. Then he starts up again.

Jesus says: Okay, okay. All right, folks. Okay. So, let me tell you a story. An illustrative kind of story. It's what us preachermen call An Illustration. And this illustration is a true story. A true story of a kid I know. A man named Reginald, Reggie for short. A sweet kid. A sweet, sad, kinda scared, little kid. Can I tell you Reggie's story?

Jesus looks right at me when he says this. I feel weird. I feel really weird because my name is Reginald. Also, I go by Reggie for short. But he can't mean me. I don't know Jesus. I mean, I know who he is, but I don't really know him. So, I don't see how he can mean me when I don't even know him.

Jesus says: This is Reggie's story. But I want you guys to think about it as if it's your own. Because even though this story is just an illustration, you might come to see that the point of any illustration is this: That when you really think about, the story, the illustration, is really about you.

II. The Illustration

THE ILLUSTRATION GOES like this: There's a little orphan kid named Reginald, or Reggie for short. Reggie wasn't always an orphan though. Reggie starts out with his parents. Then his mom dies. He doesn't know much about how she dies. The little bit that he does know is that his mom and dad had been fighting and then something happens and then his mom dies. That's all Reggie knows. But the fact is Reggie's mom and dad fought a lot. They fought a lot and most all their fights were about the same thing. Most all their fights were about affairs. And by affairs, I mean infidelity. That last fight, the last fight before his mom dies, is about Reggie's mom having had an infidelity with their local church preacher. Reggie doesn't remember that. He's too little. But that's what that last fight is about.

So, as it goes, after his mom dies, Reggie's dad leaves and he never sees his dad again, at least as far as I know, he never sees his dad again. And Reggie's alone. Not completely alone. He stays with people, family members, his grandfather, I think, adopts him or something like that. So, Reggie isn't literally, physically alone, but in his heart, he feels it. That aloneness. In his heart. He feels it.

Reggie especially feels it when the people around him are arguing, fighting. Doesn't matter what the fight is about. Reggie feels this terrible bad, nervous feeling in his stomach and, strangely, in his arms, like his arms go cold and tingly. But he never says anything, because he doesn't know what to say or who to say it to. Reggie doesn't know what to say because he doesn't understand why he feels like that, but you and I might have an idea. Because you and I might understand that Reggie's in kind of a vulnerable situation. He's an orphan. His mom's dead. His dad's gone. He's living out some kind of Oedipal nightmare from his proverbial pre-verbal childhood. Some kind of existential insecurity that he's too little to have the executive functioning to process…

Sorry, that got a little heady, but you all understand.

So, Reggie's just this ball of nerves. Just nervous and not knowing what to do about it. Stomach hurts. Arms cold. Feet and legs cold too. Head hurts. Not hurts so much as feels like he can't think, like his head can't get organized. Reggie doesn't understand why this all is happening to him. He feels like a crazy person. A crazy person pacing around the house. Not saying anything. Not knowing what to say. Just pacing around.

That's when we all come around.

We say: Reggie?

Reggie looks at us. He looks surprised to see us.

We say: What is it in your heart of hearts that you most wish for right now?

Reggie rubs the eyes on his little face.

Reggie says: I don't know.

We say: You can just say it.

Reggie says: I don't like people fighting.

We say: You want to make people not fight?

Reggie says: Yes.

We say: Why do you want to make people not fight?

Reggie says: Because it scares me.

It's sad to hear Reggie say this, but you probably wouldn't be surprised to hear that a lot of little kids say something like this. Sad, right!? So many kids scared of their parents fighting, just not feeling safe in that kind of environment. I mean, think about it! These little kids, so vulnerable. Their very lives at the mercy of their parents, or their parental substitutes.

So, so many kids have this same wish. So many that we made a protocol around how to grant this wish. The thing we do, and this is gonna make perfect sense when you hear it, the thing we do is we give these sweet little kids a kind of a super power. A gift. A talent. We give them this special talent where we turn them into a kind of an emotional fire fighter. We make it so these kids are always looking out for fire, emotional fire. Listening in, checking your face, your voice, your posture, all of that, so they can figure out how you're feeling. Then they figure out if you're upset and they jump right in with firehoses and CPR, but you understand, it's not firehoses, it's more like smiles and back pats. It's smiles and back pats and everything's all okay. I mean, all okay as far as that kind of thing is okay.

This is the thing we do for kids like Reggie. We don't ask him if he's sure. We never do that. We just ask him what he wishes for and then we just give it to him. That's the deal. And by that we abide.

III. The Highlight

ONE OF THE people sitting next to Jesus takes out a guitar and starts playing. She plays a Mumford and Sons song, not I Will Wait, but another song that I don't remember the name of. I try to figure out the name of the song, but I can't figure it out. I'm a big fan of that band, but I can't remember the name of that song. It's like my head's having a hard time organizing my thoughts. I rub my eyes. I hum along to the song. The people at the table sing along. Some of the standing people also sing along. One guy has a little basket that he carries around. Some people put money in the basket. He tells the people who don't put money that he's got the swipe thing on his phone if they need, or they can Venmo or SquareCash, if that's easier. Or even Chase, and even PayPal.

Jesus stays seated. He lifts his hands up and sways to the music. This all goes on for maybe a minute or maybe less and then the guitar player plays a sort of wrap-up riff and Jesus starts talking again.

Jesus says: Ok, friends. Let's wrap this up. Let's get to The Highlight of my message, okay? The Highlight. The Point. The Moral of the story, so to speak. So, this is it. This is The Highlight.

Everybody starts to settle down. Jesus waits for them to get organized. They redirect their attention back to Jesus.

Jesus says: So, this wish that we grant. This wish we grant for whatever it is that you want when you're still little. That wish. That wish is not the end of it.

People seem to get a little energized now. Maybe because they can tell this thing is almost over.

Jesus says: Because, that first wish, that first wish is almost always a mistake. Can you see what I mean? You always wish for the wrong thing, even though it seems like the right thing at the time. That's why we give you that wish when you're too little to know better. Not because then you'll wish for something good, but because we already know you'll wish for something bad, but you're still little, so at least you won't wish for something that's too too jacked up, you see what I mean?

There are some people now with kind of confused looks on their faces.

Jesus says: We give you that first wish then, when you're still little so as to protect you from yourselves. But that is not when it ends. There is more. Am I right? There is always more.

Jesus slowly gets up from the bench. He steps back and stands up straight. As he stands up, we can all see how big he is. He's a big man. Very, very tall and also thick, strong looking. He looks like some kind of middle-aged Korean lumberjack surfer.

He starts talking again, but quieter now. Much quieter.

Jesus says: There's a second wish.

We all lean forward to hear him.

Jesus says: And this second wish only comes to a few, just a few, and by just a few, I mean those few who didn't wish for puppies and candy. I mean those few who wished for something else. Something desperate. Those are the few who sometimes come to be ready to be little again. You get me? To be little again. To be innocent again. And the way we know that they're ready is that they've used up that first wish. They've used it all up. And it's kept them safe for a long, long time. But all that time, they didn't know it, but all that time, using that first wish, it was taking a toll on them. On their bodies, on their minds, on their hearts. Wearing them out. Using them up.

Jesus pauses and sort of takes a deep breath.

Jesus says: So, this second wish, when they get it, you want to know what? Every single one who gets that second wish, the thing is, they all wish for the same thing. The same thing. They don't wish for money, even though most of the time they could use it. They don't wish for revenge, even though most of the time they want it. They don't even wish for the end of poverty or the cure for cancer, even though those are good, good, noble things. They don't even wish for that. Do you want to know what each and every one of those that get a second wish wish for?

Most everybody nods their heads, including me.

Jesus says: They wish for the only thing that really matters. They wish for the only thing that ever really mattered. They all wish to know what it feels like to be truly and completely, unconditionally loved.

Right when he says that, I laugh out loud.

I say: Ha!

I say ha pretty loud, but nobody notices. Nobody notices except for the amen guy, the guy who said Amen at the wrong time earlier and that I then patted on the back. That guy notices. He looks at me and kind of nods. I nod back. He waves at me. I wave back. He makes a kind of a motion with his hands like he's pulling on the collar of an imaginary jacket.

The amen guy mouths the words: Aren't you hot?

I shake my head.

I mouth the words: No, I'm okay.

The person with the guitar starts to play another song. This song is a Sting song, Fields of Gold. I like that song. It's a pretty song, especially the way the person with the guitar sings it. I sort of get lost in the song for a second. The sun is setting and there is a kind of goldenness to everything. The people around Jesus start to bunch in closer. Some of them put their arms around each other. I think some of them are even crying. Actually, I'm sure of it. Some of them are definitely crying.

The amen guy starts to walk over to me. I look down and then look back up. He's still walking over to me. He waves at me. I wave back, but I also start to back away. He looks like a nice guy. I think he looks like a nice guy. But I still back away. He waves. It's a little kid wave. He waves a little kid wave and smiles at me. I nod back at him. I keep backing away.

The amen guy mouths the words: Thank you.

I nod.

The amen guy mouths the words: I'm glad you came.

I nod. I nod again. I back away. I then I turn and walk. I walk away, checking back until the amen guy stops looking at me. I'm just far enough so that it seems like I'm probably not there for the Jesus thing anymore. But I'm still close enough to see. I see Jesus. He makes his way through this little circle. He puts his hands on the amen guy. He puts his hands on the top of the head of the amen guy. He puts his hands on his shoulders. He puts his hands on the back of his neck. He leans in and says something to him. The amen guy gets emotional when Jesus does this. He starts crying and wraps his arms around Jesus. All the while, the guy with the credit card swipe and basket is going around.

IV. The Passing of the Peace

THIS ENDS AFTER a short while. It's dusk now, still enough sunlight out to keep the street lights from switching on. Most of the people leave. Jesus still hangs out. He talks to the two, three people who stay. He looks like he's praying. Then he's joking around. Then he's drinking a Diet Coke out of the can with a straw. When he's done with the Coke, he gets up from the bench and gives the few people left a hug and then starts to walk towards the street.

He walks towards a kind of fancy electric car that I don't know the name of. I follow him. He takes out the car remote and unlocks the car. I start running. I run towards him and his car. He doesn't see me running.

As he's getting in on the driver side, I open the passenger door and jump in too.

I'm sitting in the passenger seat. Jesus is sitting in the driver seat. He looks at me like he's not all that surprised. I grab my gun. I point my gun at him. He puts his hands up.

I try to say something, but I'm out of breath. I hold my hand up to him to signal for him to wait because I'm out of breath. He nods. I keep pointing the gun at him. He puts his hands down. I motion for him to put his hands back up. He puts his hands back up. I catch my breath.

I say: You fucked my wife.

Jesus says: I'm sorry. I'm not sure I know what you're talking about.

I say: You fucked my fuckin' wife, man!

Jesus keeps his hands up. He keeps his hands up and his eyes on me.

Jesus says: You're Jenny's husband.

I say: Genna! Genna, not Jenny. Genna!

I rub my face, then I quickly stop rubbing my face. I point the gun at Jesus again.

I say: You fucked my wife.

Jesus says: Well, I didn't technically fuck her.

I shake the gun in his face. He doesn't seem to freak out about this. I shake it again.

Jesus says: Okay. Let's just say I did make love to your wife.

I say: You fucked her.

Jesus says: I did not fuck her.

I say: The fuck you didn't.

I wave the gun around the car so as to say that I'm going to go crazy and shoot up Jesus and his fancy car.

Jesus says: I'm not trying to aggravate you. It's a necessary distinction. I didn't fuck Genna. I didn't fuck her. I don't fuck people.

I say: What?

Jesus says: I don't fuck people.

I say: What?

Jesus says: I'm a virgin.

I'm about to say what again, but I don't. I think he's telling the truth. Then I think he's probably a really good liar. I say, fucking shit, and Jesus smiles and I don't know why, but I'm not so mad for a second. Then I picture this big, giant, old-ass, lumberjack Jesus having sex with Genna, and I'm mad again.

I say: The fuck kind of name is Jesus?

Jesus says: It's my name. It's a very common Spanish name.

I say: You're Korean, man.

Jesus says: I'm Chinese actually.

I say: I thought you were Korean.

Jesus says: I get that a lot. Because of my face or because of my name?

I say: Name. But also face.

Jesus nods.

Jesus says: I'm glad you came today, Reggie.

I point the gun at him, really sticking it in his face now.

Jesus says: I'm sorry about your wife. But you gotta know, that's something that's been a long time coming. And you're gonna see, it's better this way. The two of you. Well, the two of you have run your course.

I don't know what to say about that.

Jesus says: What do you want, Reggie? What do you really want?

I say: I don't know.

Jesus says: You want my car? You seem to like my car.

I say: It is a nice car.

Jesus says: Okay. Let's say, I give you the car. But you sure that's what you really want?

I say: What are you doing, man! No, that's not what I said. I don't want your car.

I press the gun up against Jesus's forehead.

Jesus says: Is there something else then? What about revenge?

I keep the gun up against his head.

Jesus says: Or what about, I don't know, Genna? You want Genna back?

Jesus smiles. I think he's smiling because he's making a joke at me. But then I think he's not really making a joke at me. He's smiling because he's happy. I think that's what it is. He's smiling because he's happy.

My arm starts to get tired from holding up the gun, but I keep it held up, up to his forehead. He doesn't seem to mind though. He doesn't even seem to notice anymore that I have a gun to his head. He just smiles and looks at me. He looks me in the eyes. I can see his eyes. They're dark brown and kind of wet like he might start crying, but not the upset kind of crying, but the compassionate kind of crying.

He starts to lower his hands.

I say: Don't move.

I press the gun hard enough against his forehead to push his head back a little bit.

Jesus says: It's okay.

I say: Did Genna tell you all that about me?

Jesus says: All what?

I say: All that in The Illustration.

Jesus says: Oh, I don't know. Probably. I got so many stories. It's hard to keep track where they come from. You know what I mean?

I sort of laugh, but my mouth doesn't work right so it comes out weird.

I say: Well, that is my story.

He nods. He nods like he understands. Like he understands that it's my story. Like that's the whole reason why he told that story in the first place. The he goes on lowering his hands. He lowers his hands until he's got his hands on my shoulders. He's holding me by the shoulders. I shrug to get him to let go of my shoulders, but his hands are really strong.

The radio in the car comes on. I don't know how Jesus got the radio to come on, but it does. It comes on and there's a song I don't know, but it's a pretty song. It sounds like that Jeff Buckley Hallelujah song, but it's not. It's maybe Nick Cave. Maybe, but I don't know. But it is pretty. It's a sad pretty piano song and then a guy singing like he's also sad. But the guy's not really singing. He's sort of sing-talking. The Nick Cave sounding guy is sing-talking and the words start with something like: I don't believe in an interventionist god, but I know that you do.

I'm getting lost a little bit in the music. Meanwhile, Jesus keeps holding my shoulders steady. The way he's holding my shoulders goes well with the music. I start to realize that my shoulders have been really tight. Jesus squeezes down on my tight shoulders. I feel my shoulders go a little weak. But not a bad kind of weak. It's a good kind. Like my shoulders just relaxed for the first time in a long time.

The music gets louder. It's at the refrain, and the refrain goes: Into my arms, hold on. This repeats over and over, and now I know what song it is. It is Nick Cave. It's Nick Cave's song, Into My Arms, which is pretty much the exact right song to come on right now. I don't know how Jesus got it to play right then, but it's playing. Into My Arms by Nick Cave is playing, and I'm holding a gun to Jesus's head. I'm holding a gun to Jesus's head but my arm is tired from holding the gun to Jesus's head. I put my other hand on my gun hand to help hold the gun up, but it doesn't help. My arm is so tired.

My arm and my shoulders and really all of me. I'm just really, really tired now. I want to put the gun down. I want to put the gun down and really all of it. I want to put everything down. But then what? Then what?

Then Jesus moves his hands off my shoulders and on to my face. He's holding my face with both his hands. Cradling my face in his hands. His hands are warm and soft. Warm and soft and strong.

Jesus says: What is it you really want, Reggie? Go ahead. You can tell us. Whatever it is, whatever it is. Whatever it is in your heart of hearts that you most wish for right now?

Fugitive Traditions

a conversation with
Matvei Yankelevich

(conducted by Etan Nechin)

IN THE PARADIGM of American market-driven publishing, small presses are usually defined by a low annual turnover and limited-run editions. But Ugly Duckling Presse (UDP), disproves this narrow definition. UDP is pioneer in this pioneer tradition, beginning as a zine in the '90s and transforming into an internationally acclaimed "mission-driven small press" publishing emerging, international, and forgotten writers.

In this, UDP is part of a tradition of small presses—from Walt Whitman's self-published poem to the Soviet Samizdat—that operated under their own aesthetic and political paradigms.

Where mainstream publishing houses value wide circulation, small presses value deliberate and meaningful readership; community over ubiquity. For presses not concerned with the profit margin, it is on the margins of literature that they find their place.

UDP was founded by Matvei Yankelevich and Trista Newyear. Yankelevich, Russian-born poet, translator, and teacher, serves as the executive director of UDP.

UDP operates from the Old American Soda Factory in Gowanus, its home since 2006. The space has high ceilings, which is good, because stacked from floor to ceiling are books, boxes, papers, and printing material. Editors, interns, apprentices all share the space. The office also hosts editorial meetings, as well as educational programming, readings, letterpress events, and other creative ventures. But what stands out—its creative and ideological beating heart—is the working Heidelberg Windmill letterpress in the middle of the space.

TBLR

Let's talk about the notion of a press. If presses or publications are sometimes called houses, what kind of house is Ugly Duckling Presse? What does your home look like?

M.Y.

I LIKE TO think of UDP as an extended network of people that reflects the places I lived while running the press: from Moscow to New Haven to New York. We work as a collective: volunteers, apprentices, people who come to do one project. It's not a stable house: because the collective changes all the time there's not a lot of hierarchy; there's no "dad."

We meet four times a year with the larger collective and once a week with the four members of the core team to ensure we can fulfill the collective's vision. The collective is always changing; we have only a couple of people from the early days. I would say it's a house with open doors.

TBLR

Do you have a central working paradigm or aesthetic that guides UDP despite the constant flux of people?

M.Y.

THE GUIDING PRINCIPLE of the press is to be a space for collective work and collaboration. There's no one way of doing things; a book doesn't need to look a certain way. Aesthetics change a lot, depending on who's around. There's a lot of cross-influence. We have an apprenticeship program where apprentices learn about publishing by making books. We also help other small presses to make books.

As we work on a project, another might begin, just by sitting around the table and talking. Different people meet here: they might start a magazine together, or come up with a project for the press. For instance, we recently launched the Señal, a series of contemporary Latin American poetry.

TBLR

You publish many books from your open reading season. Is there a correlation between your changing aesthetics and what people send you over time? Is the publishing process reciprocal in that respect?

M.Y.

IN A WAY. We just had a meeting for deciding next year's books. I am always surprised at what comes out: different formats, genres, language. In the end, as a publisher, you're only as good as what people send you.

We're a mission-driven publication searching for projects and writers that have something new and surprising. Some of the projects need our help to get to where they can be. We look at the potential of a work rather than thinking if that person is well-positioned or has an established readership. It's never a discussion of salability. In that regard, we work opposite of mainstream publication, because we publish a lot of overlooked and marginalized works.

TBLR

Marginalization is a slippery term in the US of 2019. How do you define the margin in a world that is increasingly decentralized?

M.Y.

IN THE EARLY days of the press, we had this term *junior artist*. None of us had worked in publishing, we learned as we went along, and we published other people who "lacked credentials." We still gravitate to publishing people who don't necessary promote themselves and whose work doesn't fit in a particular publishing category—that's a type of margin.

I see our publication in the same tradition of small press publication in the '60s and '70s and the Mimeo Revolution, and the Language poets. It was a situation in which very marginal publishing, done by invented processes and experimentation, became a history of American poetry. You can go even further backward, to Dickenson and Whitman. A self- or marginally-published poetry that became a historical fact.

TBLR

Books as historicized objects? Isn't there a risk these works will be absorbed into the mainstream, lose their political or linguistic edge?

M.Y.

NOT NECESSARILY. YOU could say Allen Ginsburg is mainstream, but not really. His poetry still rings odd. When City Lights published *Howl*, it was definitely marginal poetry that became accepted yet did not become a center. The recognition didn't change the poetry itself: it is still antagonizing, unusual, it retains its specificity while being canonical. It was a historical change that happened in a small press culture.

It resembles what happened to us. In the late '90s we, along with magazines like *Tin House*, *Fence* and *McSweeney's*, tried to operate on the stage of noticeability. We believed poetry could be read in wider circles. But looking back, it hadn't changed things for serious poetry. That will always evade the market, because the market doesn't know how to read it.

TBLR

You have a series called Lost Literature where you publish forgotten or overlooked books. But in the age of the internet, isn't everything already unearthed?

M.Y.

BEING ONLINE IN the late '90s gave us and many small presses a platform of visibility and reach, and we still put out web-only books, talks, audio, etc. But the internet is decentralized in a way that offers few surprises; search is intentional but flat. What comes up is usually best sellers and sanctioned works. It's hard to find something out of the mainstream, especially in foreign languages.

There are a lot of books the American audience isn't exposed to, and when it is, it's under the "world literature" umbrella, which is the most easily digestible and commercially viable literature. There are sanctioned "representatives" for each country or region, like the Indian Subcontinent, African literatures, and Latin America, but what these books mostly tell is a "universal" story.

What UDP does is publish writers who are known in their literary circles but that are not necessarily gained mainstream status, whether for political reasons or other. You can see it in Post-Soviet countries: you have a literary establishment that still operates in a Soviet mindset. It's ending as time progresses.

For example, we're putting out a 300-page book of the work of Dmitri Prigov. Prigov was a dissident poet who was briefly institutionalized by the State. Although he was a dissident, you can still see the influence of Malevich and other Constructivists. He's not only a marginalized poet. He's part of Soviet poetics, and you can't understand what happened in Soviet poetry in the '70s and '80s without him.

So the books you publish serve as an education in avant-garde?

M.Y.

YES, BUT EVEN more so, we want to show that this definition can be fluid. There are many traditions of avant-garde. There are different types of marginalized groups. We're interested in fugitive, marginal traditions because of what these voices do to poetry, how they treat language, how it's being translated into English. It's not only about filling gaps for English speaking readers but hopefully, these poetries will make incursions into American poetry.

For example, we've published a book by Wingston González, a Guatemalan poet writing in Garifuna, (an Arawakan language influenced by other indigenous languages, Spanish and West African languages, mostly spoken mostly in Central America and the Caribbean). The translator, Urayoán Noel, tried to deliver the heterogeneous nature of the language into English. This goes against the monolingual tradition questioning aesthetics in English language poetry.

TBLR

Looking through your catalogue, I see a lot of poetry, hybrid forms, artist books, but hardly any novels. Is it because of the manuscripts you receive or is there a resistance to fiction?

M.Y.

WE HAVE A few fiction titles, but we publish very sparingly. Our structure is geared towards poetry. Other literary publishers have better apparatuses to make a novel succeed. There are exceptions, of course. We published *Modern Love*, a book by artist Constance DeJong from 1977, and it has found an audience. Then again, it's not a typical novel.

Beyond structural issues, a novel is already a particular Western form into which one can write from anywhere and is easily replicated. The novel is susceptible to being universalized. Of course a novel could be about a specific location, but it is concerned with plot for the most part—actions the words convey instead of the words themselves. Because poetry foregrounds language, if it's paying attention to itself, it imbues a specific locality; it's nationally or linguistically bound. The way poetry reacts to the present doesn't conform to a single space or form.

TBLR

You're also a translator. [Yankelevich has translated numerous works from Russian, including two books by Daniil Kharms, *Incidences* and *Today I Wrote Nothing.*] *Do you have a different sensitivity as a publisher who also translates?*

M.Y.

WE PUBLISH TEN percent of all poetry in translation in the US. This just shows the dire situation of works in translation. American publishing has a problematic stance in regards to works in translation. The goal of mainstream publishers for the most part is to make readers feel like they have complete access to the original work. They obfuscate "foreignness." In many cases the name of the translator doesn't appear on the cover, and some translators don't receive copyright.

American culture either ignores or is suspicious of translation. Translators are double agents and spies—*traduttore, traditore*, as the Italian saying goes. But choices of language carry certain consequences and the people who make these choices are hidden. Most of the public doesn't know who translates, for example, Elena Ferrante. In popular novels, it's easier to get away with because with a story, although it may be narratively complicated, the texture of its language is single-layered.

TBLR

And in poetry?

M.Y.

TRANSLATING A POEM is a limit case of translation, where it tests its own boundaries, dealing with the loss and gain of meaning, with transcreation. It gives us access, but also reveals the spaces that are closed to us, to another culture or language. Derrida compares translation to a ruin: you have an imagination of what it was like, but it is the loss that's visible.

TBLR

So translation reveals temporality?

M.Y.

YES. READING A poem in translation is like an echo, a voice that's simultaneously present and removed. You engage with a translation not only on the page but also by beginning to make different speculations about time and space. It makes you question the effects you're experiencing. It is an act of reconstruction from particles of memory.

TBLR

And preserving the foreignness of the piece?

M.Y.

IN WORKS THAT are more particular or minor, choices of language become more crucial. I think of Kafka in this regard. Kafka's work springs from writing in a language not his own. It distorts the writing in a particular way. Choices of translation then, have to do not only with language but Kafka's cultural situation. He was writing in the margins of an empire and reflecting the Empire's language to it. That's why although he's canonical, his writing still avoids the mainstream. He keeps on being an outlier; that's what keeps making his writing fresh.

TBLR

The outlier as a foreigner?

M.Y.

OR IMMIGRANT. VILÉM Flusser wrote about how the immigrant or exile disturbs the idea of a home for the people living in it. This because the immigrant has set themself free from the habits of their homeland and has yet to adopt the practices of the adopted home. You can see it in Clarice Lispector, another immigrant to Brazil. She handled Portuguese in a completely different way because of her vantage point.

It's interesting to me because of my background, moving from the Soviet Union, and adopting a new language. I grew up in a microcosm of Jewish dissident intelligentsia who still saw themselves as the intellectual elite even though they were marginal to the US. I was always interested in what displacement does to writing, how it retains its foreignness, whether it's Kafka, Paul Celan, or Bruno Schulz.

TBLR

Do you mean minor literatures?

M.Y.

I MEAN WRITING that's not interested in heroism. You can say that Jane Bowls, Jean Rhys, or even Virginia Woolf fit that category because their work is concerned with subjective spaces. In the case of poetry, it's work that doesn't try to master the language, like Lowell or Merrill, it just examines different possibilities.

TBLR

You publish a lot of writers whose work has been suppressed or outwardly marginalized by their governments. In the US, this didn't happen. Is there a different set of consequences for poetry in a free market society?

M.Y.

I THINK THERE are similarities in avant-garde traditions in that regard. Of course, Aram Saroyan wasn't suppressed for publishing his one-word poems in George Plimpton's magazine. But it was ridiculed, and there was a public outcry about funding he received from the National Endowment for the Arts. The rationale was, *if no one is reading it, why should we pay for it?* This attitude shows how the public has internalized market ideology. Saroyan suffered public scrutiny like Robert Mapplethorpe and others. This distortion and flattening of culture worked: since the '80s and '90s, federal funding for the arts has dwindled, there are fewer spaces to read and publish, and fewer libraries have open stacks.

In 1998, there was an exhibition in the New York Public Library that documented the small press scene in New York and San Francisco. In the book that accompanied the show, *Secret Location on the Lower Side* (Granary Books), Jerome Rothenberg wrote that class divide and poets, writers, and publishers living on the margins of society propelled this movement, and it was public spaces and resources that nurtured it. Rather than being suppressed by the State, American poets are marginalized by the corporatized power structures.

I don't think any avant-garde poet has an expectation of becoming a career writer. They just want a space to publish their poems and a place where they can interact with other writers and readers. Things did change a bit in the '90s when hiring in universities became more diverse and a career could be made by being published in magazines. But for the most part, poetry from the avant-garde tradition was never published in Norton or Penguin. The doors are still, for the most part, controlled by official verse culture.

TBLR

So UDPs collective, collaborative structure, and the fact that you have a working letterpress is a way to resist this hegemonic apparatus?

M.Y.

YES. OWNING YOUR means of production makes you more autonomous. We are one of the few presses that has its editorial office, letterpress, and nonprofit headquarters all in the same space. This makes it easier to get projects going, involve educational programming, and put out material.

It's like the DIY culture we grew out of in the '90s. Zines were important because of how they were made and to whom they were circulated. It was a network of people that showed different possibilities of writing and producing alternative culture. We try to carry this spirit into the press. If I wanted to print a poem or make a poster for a political rally I could probably just typeset the press and do it in one night. We actually want to bring one of those old Xerox machines to the office. The simpler, the better.

TBLR

This tradition carries with it a certain political discourse? Not left or right, but the way these presses imbue politics?

M.Y.

DEFINITELY. POLITICS INCLUDES the type of paper used, the mode of distribution, all really telling of the politics of the organization. In that regard, the politics of Random House is very clear from the way their books are made. The politics are embodied in the aesthetics. The content doesn't need to be political, but the way it comes out to the world is political.

Diane DiPrima wrote in *Revolutionary Letters*, "This is a free book. These are free poems and may be reprinted anytime by anyone... Power to the people's Mimeo Machines." When you can edit, print, and publicize, without institutional forces that bend you into conformity, your options expand. I think all our books have politics in the way we put them out and reflect back on what we are as a house. In the end, our house is made up of all the desires of the people who work here and the constraints we come up against. Which, come to think of it, is a lot like translation.

Contributors

Anna Andrew is a South Sudanese writer based in Egypt. Ms. Andrew was born in 1962 in the village of Magwi, Eastern Equatoria, and since 2002 has sought refuge in Cairo with her family. Ms. Andrew specializes in hybrid cuisine with emphasis on freshness and healthy diet. "Five Ways to Eat Termites" is her first publication.

Catharina Coenen is a first-generation German immigrant to the northwestern "chimney" of Pennsylvania, where she teaches biology at Allegheny College. Much of her creative work addresses transgenerational effects of war. Over the past year, her essays have appeared in *The American Scholar*, *The Southampton Review Online*, *Superstition Review*, *Appalachian Heritage*, *Christian Science Monitor*, The *Flash Nonfiction Food* anthology published by Woodhall Press, and elsewhere.

Catherine C. Con grew up in Taiwan. She earned a B.A. in English Literature from Fu-Jen Catholic University in Taipei and an MS in Information Systems from Louisiana State University in Baton Rouge. She is a Computer Science instructor at University of South

Carolina, Upstate. Her short story "A Tale of Two Paintings" was published in *Emrys Journal* in 2019 and nominated for a 2020 PEN American Literary Award. Her flash non-fiction "Birthday" will be published in *Tint Journal*, Fall 2019. Her short story "Janus" was published in *The Petigru Review*. Her nonfiction "This Writing Life" is forthcoming in *Emrys Journal* in 2020.

Chekwube Danladi is a writer and a reformed punk. Her debut collection, *Semiotics*, is the winner of the 2019 Cave Canem Poetry Prize, and is forthcoming from the University of Georgia Press in Fall 2020. She lives in Chicago.

Siyun Fang is a poet and translator. A graduate of Centre College and New York University, she is currently attending The New School MFA Program. Her poems have appeared in *Rigorous*, *Tule Review*, *In Parentheses*, and *Seven CirclePress*, among other journals and magazines. Her research interests include modern and contemporary poetry, poetic theories, theories of narrative, American fiction, as well as dramatic arts.

Josey Foo is the author of *A Lily Lilies* (with Leah Stein) from Nightboat Books 2011, and *Tomie's Chair* from Kaya/Muae 2002. She is Malaysian of multi-ethnic descent—Hakka, Nyonya-Peranakan, and Thai. The Hakka ("guest people") experienced great internal migrations in China for more than 2,000 years, and in the mid-1800s became overseas migrants, building the last stretch of the Transcontinental Railroad and laboring on mines and plantations. Raised in several Malaysian cities, she attended college in the United States, followed by a few years of undocumented status, working odd jobs in New York City. In the last 20 years she has worked in law and grassroots organizing on the Navajo Nation. She is a 2001 recipient of a Literature Fellowship from the National Endowment for the Arts.

Jamaican-born **Donna Hemans** is the author of the novels *River Woman* and *Tea by the Sea*, which will be published in June 2020 by Red Hen Press. In 2015, she won the Lignum Vitae Una Marson

Award for Adult Literature for the unpublished manuscript of *Tea by the Sea*. Her short stories and essays have appeared in *Vol. 1 Brooklyn*, *Caribbean Writer*, *Crab Orchard Review*, *Witness*, *The Millions*, and *Scoundrel Time*, among others. She has won grants from Black Mountain Institute, Millay Colony and Virginia Center for the Creative Arts in support of her work. Find her online at donnahemans.com or on Twitter @donna_hemans.

Pete Hsu is a first-generation Taiwanese American writer in Los Angeles. His stories have appeared in *The Los Angeles Review*, AAWW's *The Margins*, *F(r)iction Magazine*, and others. He is a former PEN America Emerging Voices Fellow and PEN in the Community's Writer in Residence. He holds a BA in English Literature from UCLA and is the Fiction Editor for *Angels Flight * literary west*. For more, please see: peterhzhsu.com

Mehdi M. Kashani lives and writes in Toronto, Canada. His fiction and nonfiction can be found in *The Rumpus*, *Catapult*, *The Fiddlehead*, *The Malahat Review*, *Wigleaf*, *Bellevue Literary Review*, *Four Way Review*, *The Minnesota Review*, *Emrys Journal* (for which he won 2019 Sue Lile Inman Fiction Award), among others. To learn more about him, visit his website: mehdimkashani.com

Etan Nechin is the online editor of The Bare Life Review, and an Israeli writer. His writing has appeared in *Zyzzyva*, *Apogee*, *The Forward*, *Ha'aretz*, *Columbia Journal*, *Huffington Post*, *Entropy*, and more. His text "UTTER" was performed at the 2015 Venice Biannale. He is a recipient of the Felipe De Alba Award for Fiction.

Sergio Aguilar Rivera is a writer born in Hidalgo, Mexico and raised in Bay Point, California. He is a graduate of the Iowa Writers' Workshop and is currently working on a novel.

Anca Roncea grew up in Romanian, speaks Modern Greek, French, and writes in English. She was born in Romania under communism and raised in a Post-Communist Romania transitioning to capitalism. She has lived in Bucharest, Iowa City, Yangon, Los Angeles,

Paris and is currently in New York. Through her work she explores the space where language can create pivots in the midst of displacement while incorporating the aesthetics of Constantin Brancusi and the women artists of the Dada Movement. She is a graduate of the Iowa Writers' Workshop, the UIowa Literary Translation MFA program and her work can be found in the *Berkeley Poetry Review*, *Beecher's Magazine*, *Omniverse and Asymptote*, *The Bare Life Review* and the upcoming issue of *Lana Turner*.

Jehad Saftawi is a photojournalist and videographer who's currently based in the bay area, California. His work covers the daily life in the Gaza Strip, shining a spotlight on human rights abuses.

Namwali Serpell is a Zambian writer who teaches at the University of California, Berkeley. She won the 2015 Caine Prize for African Writing. She received a Rona Jaffe Foundation Writers' Award for women writers in 2011 and was selected for the Africa39, a 2014 Hay Festival project to identify the best African writers under 40. Her first novel, *The Old Drift* (Hogarth/PRH, 2019), was long listed for the Center for Fiction First Novel Prize and described by Salman Rushdie in *The New York Times Sunday Book Review* as "a dazzling debut, establishing Namwali Serpell as a writer on the world stage."

Jesus Francisco Sierra emigrated from Cuba in 1969 to San Francisco's Mission District. He is a member of the Advisory Council at The Writers Grotto where he is working on a collection of short stories set in Havana during the early days of the Revolution and contemporary San Francisco. His work has appeared in *Zyzzyva*, *Lunch Ticket*, *Marathon Literary Review*, *The Acentos Review* and *Gulf Stream Literary Journal* among others. His personal essays "How Baseball Saved My Life" and "Soul Music," which initially appeared in Lunch Ticket, have been anthologized in the recently published *Endangered Species, Enduring Values: An Anthology of San Francisco Area Writers of Color*. He is fascinated by how transitions, both sought and imposed, have the power to either awaken or suppress the spirit. He is a licensed Structural Engineer and holds an MFA in Fiction from Antioch University Los Angeles.

Liwa Sun is a Chinese writer, poet, and a game-theorist-wannabe. She lets poetry contaminate her memory, in which she rejoices. She lives in Philadelphia with a small couch and mountains of books.

Matvei Yankelevich is a poet and translator and one of the founding editors of Ugly Duckling Presse, a nonprofit publisher of poetry, translation, performance texts, and books by artists, based in Brooklyn. He curates UDP's Eastern European Poets Series, and was a co-editor of the poetry journal *6x6* from 2000 to 2017. His poetry books include *Some Worlds for Dr. Vogt* (Black Square, 2015); his translations include *Today I Wrote Nothing: The Selected Writings of Daniil Kharms* (Ardis/Overlook, 2009). He has received fellowships from the National Endowment for the Arts and the New York Foundation for the Arts. He teaches translation and book arts at Columbia University's School of the Arts and is a member of the Writing Faculty at the Milton Avery Graduate School of the Arts at Bard College.